The Traveler

The Traveler

Jennifer Deaver

atmosphere press

To my children,
Because the world needs a little more wonder

For my husband, parents, and family,
Thank you for encouraging me to follow my dreams

Chapter 1

"Annabelle, you stay inside! The wind is so strong that the peasants are blowing away!"

"Yes, Aunt Ester," Annabelle called back, shoving her bedroom window open and stepping outside onto the roof.

The wind was howling fiercely. It whipped Annabelle's dark chestnut hair around her face. She braced her hand against the window frame and watched the majesty of the mighty wind shake the leaves from the trees, moving them in little whirlwinds around the yard. Her horses ran playfully through the pastures, enjoying the wildness of the wind, their nostrils flared with excitement. She smiled to herself. Annabelle connected the most with her horses; their wild spirits always bonded closely to her caged soul.

From her rooftop, Annabelle could see past the crumbling stone courtyard walls into the capital city of the kingdom, Pelland. She watched the townspeople hunt down their loose belongings and children before the wind whisked them away. Annabelle's rooftop towered over their cream-colored cottages, all neatly lined down the cobblestone roads. Annabelle yearned to feel a part of the town, but the stone walls that were built to protect the castle, her home, were just one of many things that isolated her from the outside world.

Suddenly, a huge gust of wind came and pulled Annabelle's feet off the roof and pushed her up into the air. Annabelle reached inside the window to grab something to stabilize herself, only to find herself clutching her paisley patterned umbrella. "Sure hope this works!" Annabelle said to herself, slowly letting go of the window and opening her umbrella.

The wind pulled her up off her roof, over her castle, and carried her into the sky. She hooked the curve of her umbrella handle under her leg and watched nervously as her feet brushed past her childhood climbing tree; the old rope tree swing that was once tied to a branch had been wrapped tightly around the trunk. As a young adult now, it had been years since she took the time to touch the chipping bark on that old tree. Annabelle tried to catch one of the branches with her legs but only managed to lose one of her red shoes in the process.

Annabelle was now above the town, still several feet higher than the rooftops. Looking over her shoulder, she could see some of the small shops that butted up against the courtyard walls. The wind blew the smell of the bakery around, making her stomach growl. Even in bad weather, the shop owners were still at work. Next to the bakery, the dark grey smoke of the blacksmith's shop bellowed out of the chimney. She smiled to herself as her eyes caught sight of a small candy shop that her father used to take her to.

As she went farther through Pelland, Annabelle was

surprised to see how much the town had grown since the last time she had visited. Newly built cottages stretched out beyond the cobblestone roads, dirt paths and lumber were laid out in anticipation of even more building.

Pelland was beautiful. Gardeners carefully planted beds of brightly colored tulips and yellow daffodils. Pink and white flowering trees lined the stone roads in front of the cottages. Annabelle wondered to herself how many people saw under her petticoats. Looking wistfully at the town below, it seemed she had been unnoticed. She spent most of her life behind the castle walls, under the strict and watchful eye of her Aunt Ester. The only adventures Annabelle was allowed to have were those found in the books in the castle library.

Annabelle's Aunt Ester had always kept a close eye on her. She was never allowed to venture out of the castle, which made her feel lonely and isolated. Her father, the King, was gone frequently, and Ester was not the warm motherly type. Annabelle was treated more like a naïve child than the blossoming young woman that she was becoming.

Soon the wind blew Annabelle over the old stone walls that marked the end of Pelland. Tangled vines were slowly strangling the grey stone. She was now above the woods. Her arms ached from holding onto her umbrella so tightly.

She closed her eyes. She was very tired and was starting to get lost. She prayed silently that she would land safely and find her way back home quickly before her aunt realized what had happened to her.

Chapter 2

The bell rang loudly in Ann's ears. She opened her eyes and lifted her head up off her school desk only to see her math teacher's eyes meeting her own. "Ugh," Ann thought to herself, "another rough morning with Mr. Pothoven and his calculus."

"Ms. Lexington, do you find my teaching boring? I don't think you have been on time to any of my classes this term. You just pop in unnoticed, looking exhausted." Mr. Pothoven's eyes were full of concern and frustration.

"N-no, Mr. Pothoven . . . err . . . sorry," Ann said, her eyes studying the old, yellowed tile floor in an effort to not meet his. She could feel her freckled cheeks grow hot as she blushed in embarrassment. "I'm just not a morning person is all . . ."

"Well, alright then," Mr. Pothoven said. "Best you get to your next class before you're late."

"Okay. . . . Thank you," Ann said, grabbing her textbook off her desk and slinging her paisley patterned backpack over her shoulder. She quickly walked out of the classroom, avoiding Mr. Pothoven's eyes once again.

Her stomach felt heavy—she hated feeling like a disappointment to anyone, even her math teacher. Ann wondered to herself why she had been so tired. A good night's sleep had been eluding her the past week or so, making morning classes the worst.

When school was over Ann said goodbye to her friends and walked to the parking lot. She threw her school bag into the passenger seat of her old, red, beat-up pickup truck and headed home for the weekend. Her mind was off and wandering, her heart felt lost.

The sun was shining brightly as Ann drove through town on her way home. She stopped at the lone flashing stoplight located on the square. Dirksen's Café on the corner was already filling up with her classmates that gathered there every Friday evening for their famous ice cream. Just outside of town, she turned down the gravel road next to her friend Noah's house. She slowed to wave, seeing Noah and his dad already outside doing their daily farm chores.

"What is my purpose here?" she said aloud to herself as she drove on. Her heart felt detached. Ann ached to find her purpose in life, her reason for being. She wished to do more with her life than to feel rooted to a small town. Graduation was in a few weeks and Ann promised herself that she would go see the world, exploring lands she never imagined she would be able to. The thought of her mother sat heavily on her mind. It was hard to imagine leaving her mother behind. After dad left when she was ten, Ann was all she had.

Ann turned down another gravel road, startling some grazing cattle. She had to slow down to follow behind a green-and-yellow tractor pulling a grain cart. Her truck crept behind the tractor until she was able to turn down the winding lane to her house. Her truck kicked up dust from the dry dirt road. Fences lined either side of the lane, marking the end of the horse pastures.

She pulled into her driveway alongside a withered old oak tree. She waited a minute for the dust to settle before stepping out of her truck. She left her keys in the ignition; no need to worry about anyone stealing her old truck way out in the middle of nowhere. Ann grabbed her bag and studied her family's house, an old, white, colonial-style home with black shutters. Her mother grew up in this house, and, as she always told Ann, hoped someday her grandchildren would grow up here as well. Suddenly Ann realized her mother was peeking out of one of the living room windows, waving excitedly. Ann grinned, waved back, and headed inside.

Her mother greeted her warmly with a hug and a kiss on the cheek at the front entrance of their house. After a little small talk about school and her friends, Ann told her mother she wanted a quick nap before getting to some homework and chores. Ann left her school bag sitting by the front door and hustled upstairs into her room. She curled up in a ball in her warm and cozy bed and quickly dozed off.

Chapter 3

Annabelle woke up just as the wind started to settle down. The sun was still shining brightly; she guessed it was mid-afternoon. Annabelle thought of the dream she just had. It was of her mother, or what she imagined her mom would look like. Annabelle frequently had vivid dreams of her, in a place that seemed very different from here, full of strange technology and transportation that didn't require horses.

Annabelle was lower to the ground now, just inches above the thinning trees. She could see a narrow road ahead of her. A nearby branch caught her dress and pulled her out of the air, bringing her flight to an abrupt halt. As she fell, Annabelle let go of her umbrella and frantically grabbed for branches to slow her fall. The sound of her dress ripping and the wind in her ears was all that she could hear when she finally hit the ground with a thud. Annabelle let out a sigh of relief. It was good to be back on the ground. Her new dress was ripped and dirty. There was no way to hide this adventure from her Aunt Ester now, especially with one of her shoes lost. As she pulled a few leaves out of her terribly windblown hair, she readjusted her dress, grabbed her umbrella out of the tree, and headed toward the road she had seen. Annabelle hoped it would lead her to a nearby town.

The dust on the road stirred around her feet as she walked. The sparse shade provided by the trees was no relief to the blazing sun that shone directly above Annabelle. She hummed quietly to herself to keep her mind busy and make the time go faster.

After what seemed like hours, the trees cleared, and she could see a village about a quarter of a mile away. Annabelle grinned to herself; she was very thirsty and the thought of a cool drink of water made her walk a little faster. She squinted to get a better look at the village. The afternoon sun glinted off the ripples of a pond. Annabelle could see a welcoming dock where a young boy was perched. She guessed he was fishing. A large rust-colored barn sat close behind the pond. The houses and shops that speckled the flat land had straw rooftops. A stunning red-and-brown brick mansion stood in the distance. Annabelle smiled, as she now knew where she was. Her father had talked about Emerson's Town frequently. Emerson was a mayor, running one of the towns in her father's kingdom.

She heard a clatter behind her, coming up fast. Annabelle turned to see what the racket was. "Look out!" A sandy-blonde haired boy shouted as he pushed past her, knocking her off her feet into the dirt. There was a very feisty, angry-looking black horse tailing closely behind him.

"Jeez!" Annabelle said, getting up and brushing the dirt off her already terribly torn dress. She watched as the black mare reared in defiance of the boy. "It would have been nice to meet you about a mile or two ago," Annabelle said to herself. She studied the boy. He was maybe twelve, dressed in dirty brown pants and a tan shirt with a ripped right sleeve.

"Grab the other rope!" the boy shouted, gesturing his head toward a rope trailing behind the mare. "Hurry up now!"

Annabelle raised her eyebrows in surprise at his demand. She had never been told what to do by a peasant. She quickly hustled over and grabbed the other rope, holding tightly to it as the mare threw her head up in one last attempt to break free. The rope burned in her soft, uncalloused hands.

The horse's eyes were wide with fear. Her nostrils flared from the exertion. She was breathing heavily, and her sleek black coat was slimy with sweat. "Easy, easy, girl," Annabelle called, reaching her free hand out to the horse's nose. Annabelle's voice caught the horse's attention. The mare's black ears perked forward, and she brought her head down to Annabelle's hand.

"Hello there," Annabelle said, running her hand up and down the horse's forehead.

"Well, looks like you have her attention," the boy said. "Now bring her to the main barn and get her washed off."

Annabelle raised her eyebrows once again at the boy. "Main barn?" Annabelle realized there was no way he knew who he was talking to.

"Don't play ignorant. She's calmed down. She'll be fine as long as you don't get her all wound up again," the boy said, handing Annabelle the other lead rope and walking toward the small barn they were approaching.

Annabelle stood with both lead ropes in her hand and

her mouth open in confusion. She wasn't sure where to go or what to do with the horse. She considered trying to take the horse and ride back home, but she wasn't sure which way home was or if this horse was willing to be ridden. She looked down at her rope-burned hands and when she looked up there was a tall, blonde-haired girl about her age standing in front of her.

"Did Alec give you that mare? We'd best take it to the barn before she decides to go wild again," the young woman said, brushing a strand of her blonde hair away from her face and taking one of the lead ropes out of Annabelle's hands.

"Err. . . . I guess so," Annabelle said, allowing the young woman to lead her and the horse to the rust-colored barn. "I'm Annabelle," Annabelle said, looking over the horse to peer at the young woman on the other side. "I'm not from around here. I'm the princess. I need to get back to the castle in Pelland. I was hoping to go home before it gets dark. . . . My aunt is going to kill me."

"Ha," the blonde girl said, grinning to herself. "The castle in Pelland, huh. . . . You are quite the dreamer. I'm Whitney. I have been caring for Emerson's horses for five years now."

"Five years?" Annabelle asked, "How old are you?"

"I'm eighteen. My parents sent me here after primary school. Our family was short on money and my older brother was already here. I was hoping if I came here Alec would not have to miss school. This would have been his last year at school. . . . But he is learning how to work hard here. The guards favor him because of his hard work, and that will help him in the long run."

Annabelle thought about working at age thirteen. The

hardest job Annabelle ever had to do was sit through castle meetings. She suddenly understood what the lower classes of people had to do to survive. She worried about her own freedoms, sneaking out at night just because her aunt told her not to be out past a certain time; just little things to ensure she still could do what she wanted to. She decided not to share the truth about her being from the castle. Apparently, people wouldn't believe what she said anyway. Her hair was a mess, her dress was torn, and she had kicked off her one remaining shoe when she was walking down the dirt road. There was no way people would believe she was who she claimed to be.

They entered the barn to see beautifully built stables full of horses. Each one nickered at Whitney as they walked past. Whitney pulled a small, withered carrot out of her apron pocket and handed it to one of the horses in a nearby stall.

"Let's put her in here for now. Hopefully it will hold her this time." Whitney pulled the stall door open, leading the black mare inside. The sheen on her coat was still brilliant in the dimly lit barn. Her dark eyes settled on Annabelle again. Annabelle rubbed the mare's forehead one last time as Whitney took the rope off and shut the stall door. "So, are you a maid in the house or are you doing stall work? I can't say I've ever seen you before."

"I actually was just passing through. I really am from Pelland. I need to get back by tonight," Annabelle said, rubbing her hands together, still quite sore from the rope burn.

Whitney nodded her head in thought. They walked in silence for a bit, heading toward the back of the barn. Every nook and corner was full of old wagon parts and horse tack. Saddles and blankets for the horses lined the walls. Whitney opened up a side door and they walked inside. The small room was dimly lit. In a corner was a little cot with a lavender-colored quilt draped over it. A shelf in the corner held rows of neatly folded clothes. Books stacked in a pile sat on the nightstand that was close to the cot. Tacked to the walls were beautiful sketches of flowers and horses.

"Well, that's quite a long trip on foot," Whitney said. "My older brother has to pass through there to sell some things at the Pelland market tomorrow afternoon. It might be smarter to ride there with him than to try and travel on foot." Whitney grabbed a new tan apron and a long pale-blue dress, similar to the one she already wore, off the shelf. "Change into this first. It won't look very appropriate to be walking around in such dirty clothes. I will see if Merry Anne will fix these and have them ready for you to wear tomorrow. I will wait outside." And with that, Whitney stepped outside and shut the door.

Annabelle changed in the dark room and rolled up her dress and petticoat into a ball. The musty smell of the hay filtered through the barn and sat heavily in her lungs. She paused once more to study a sketch of a field of daisies before opening the door to see not only Whitney but a middle-aged woman with long, silvery-grey braided hair as well.

"This is Merry Anne," Whitney said, taking Annabelle's dress out of her hands and handing it to Merry Anne. "She will mend your dress and show you where you will be staying. If you need anything from me, I will be around this barn almost all the time."

"Thank you," Annabelle said with a grateful smile. She

followed Merry Anne away from the barn toward a small stone cottage on the edge of the woods. Her feet were heavy. She didn't realize how tired this journey had made her. The sun was setting, and the birds were settling down in the trees to sleep for the night. Fireflies were starting to light up the nearby pastures, and the stillness of the evening made Annabelle even more tired, but her soul was at peace here.

"You look exhausted," Merry Anne said, opening the door to her cottage. "Please, rest while I make us some supper." Merry Anne walked Annabelle into the spare bedroom and shut the door behind her as she left. Annabelle sat heavily on the bed. She curled up under the quilt and was asleep before her head even hit the pillow.

Chapter 4

Ann woke up and stretched. She still felt as tired as she had before she laid down to rest. She let her mind replay the dream she just had, of the crazy wind and a huge barn full of horses. Ann shook away the thoughts of the dream. Her alarm clock read 7:30 PM; she had slept longer than she had planned to. Ann looked at her fat and lazy grey-striped cat, Cleo, who lay on her feet. She pulled her legs out from under Cleo and put them on the floor, digging her toes into the white shag carpet. Cleo scowled, her eyes scolding Ann for disturbing her and scurried off Ann's bed and out of the room. Ann decided it was best to do her chores and get some homework done before suppertime. She stretched once more and pulled herself out of bed.

On her way down the stairs Ann noticed that she had dirt on her feet. "Strange . . . ," she thought to herself. She had worn flip-flops to school, but she didn't remember getting dirty at any point in the day. "Maybe when I got out of my truck . . . ," she thought to herself again, brushing off the thought and following her nose into the kitchen where something wonderful was baking.

Ann's mother greeted her with a smile. She was pulling a tray of chocolate chip cookies out of the oven. "You slept late. How was your nap?"

"I still feel like I haven't slept in days," Ann said, eyeing a cookie that was cooling on the counter. "It's probably just from the stress of school and finals coming up."

"Hmm," Ann's mom said, not reassured. "Well, take some time off from working with your horse before finals and take it easy. You seem exhausted." Ann reached out and snagged the cookie. It was hot in her hands, but the warm melted chocolate was just what her stomach craved.

Her mom replied with disapproving eyes. "These are for my work's coffee time, missy."

Ann grinned. "Oh, alright, mom. Sorry . . ." Ann grabbed another cookie and quickly ate it while her mother's back was turned. "I'm off to feed the horse." Ann grabbed her gum boots on her way out the door and walked quickly to the barn, only slowing to pull her long brown hair up into a ponytail and put a dusty gum boot on each foot. When she opened up the barn door, a warm nicker welcomed her. "Hello, Lucy," Ann said as she reached up and rubbed the white blaze of the horse's muzzle. The horse vigorously rubbed her head against Ann's hand through the stall door. Ann pulled a blue-and-white lead rope off the door and slid the latch open. She slipped inside and clipped the lead rope onto Lucy's halter. "Ready to ride, old girl?" Ann said with a smile.

She led Lucy out of the barn and into their pasture. She lined her up against the wood fence and climbed onto

Lucy's back. The feeling of riding bareback always made Ann's spirit fly. It was hard to hold on with her gum boots on, but she did the best she could, digging her fingers into Lucy's dark brown mane, and wrapping her legs tightly around her chestnut body. Ann ducked against Lucy as they brushed past low hanging tree branches.

As they neared the open pasture, Lucy started off at a slow lope but was spooked by a deer jumping over the fence of the pasture. She reared up, throwing her head back and hitting Ann's forehead. Ann fell off Lucy and landed hard on the ground. She curled up in a ball, black spots filling her vision. She tried to take a deep breath to stop herself from fainting, but her hearing faded, and she quickly blacked out.

Chapter 5

Annabelle woke up to the sound of rain. She slowly stretched and stood up. She must have slept too long; her head hurt, and her body was sore. She walked out of the spare room. She didn't see Merry Anne anywhere, so she took a step outside. Black clouds engulfed the evening sky, and thunder rolled through the forest around the cottage. Annabelle loved storms. The wild winds and the sound of rain, the smell of wet grass and the stillness that followed. Her Aunt Ester never let her go outside to feel the wet grass between her toes. Annabelle dug her toes into the soggy grass. She smiled to herself. She loved her aunt dearly. Her father was always gone searching for something and Ester would always keep a close eye on her while he was away. Ester always told Annabelle she was just trying to keep her safe. Her father would never talk about Annabelle's mother, nor would Ester. Ester was the only mother she had known, but she had a hard heart and was very stern. She constantly had a scowl on her face and a harsh voice that was very demanding.

Annabelle watched in the distance as a little wagon

pulled into the rust-colored barn. The horse looked tired, and the person driving was soaked from the rain.

"Good evening!" Merry Anne said, coming out through the cottage door. "It looks like they've got the wagon stocked to go to Pelland tomorrow." Merry Ann wrapped a shawl around Annabelle's shoulders. "You're going to get sick in the rain. Come inside, and I'll make you a cup of tea. Dinner should be ready soon, and this storm should pass by morning." Merry Anne took Annabelle's arm and led her back inside and into the tiny kitchen. "How did you sleep?"

Annabelle smiled as she took a seat at the table. "Just fine, thank you. I dreamed of riding a horse bareback in a pasture, and I fell off." Annabelle rubbed her forehead. The dream was so realistic, she woke up with a headache. She watched Merry Anne get the pot of tea ready. The older woman's withered hands had seen a lot of work in her lifetime. She had smile lines on both sides of her mouth and very youthful blue-grey eyes. She moved quickly to get things together. Her body was old, but Annabelle could tell that her spirit was still very young.

"Tell me about yourself, Merry Anne," Annabelle said. "Whitney didn't tell me much."

"Well, there isn't too much to tell." Merry Anne wiped her hands on her apron and sat in the chair across from Annabelle. "I grew up pretty close to here. My family raised goats and cows. I still have a few goats. They are wonderful little creatures. I have three great children. My son, Jesse, is the only one left in my house though. The rest have grown and left to find their own lives." A long pause followed, as if she were lost in thought.

"But you have no husband to take care of you?"

Annabelle asked, sitting up a little in her chair.

"No, not for many years," Merry Anne said, a smile slowly coming to her face. "There was a time when I was married, but there just wasn't a man that could keep up with me and my life." Merry Anne stopped at that, and the way she said it gave Annabelle the hint that there wasn't much else to tell. "The tea is ready," Merry Anne said, standing up from the table. "Best to drink it while it's still hot."

Merry Anne poured them each a cup and then walked over to the fireplace. She lifted the lid off the large black kettle that was hanging over the crackling fire and stirred the boiling soup. "Perfect timing, the rabbit stew is ready as well." Merry Anne filled two bowls to the brim.

Annabelle's stomach growled. The smell of the stew made her mouth water. "Nothing beats stew on a rainy day," she said, holding the warm bowl in her hands.

"It's a family recipe, I hope you like it."

Annabelle took a bite. It was so hot that it burned the roof of her mouth. "It's truly the best stew I have eaten," Annabelle replied, blowing on her stew to cool it before shoveling another spoonful in her mouth. "The carrots and celery really add to it."

Annabelle and Merry Anne enjoyed their meal as they listened to the rain splatter against the cottage roof. The little kitchen felt so warm and welcoming; Annabelle was thankful to be there. She finished her stew, stood, and stretched. "I can take your bowl if you're finished," Annabelle said as she picked up the empty dishes and put them on the counter. "Thank you for your hospitality."

"Guests are always welcome here; it is truly my pleasure," Merry Anne said. "You had better get some rest, the morning will come early."

"That sounds like a great plan. Good night, Merry Anne," Annabelle said, pushing her chair against the table and walking back to the bedroom she had napped in. With a stomach full of rabbit stew, she quickly fell back to sleep.

Chapter 6

Ann slowly sat up. She could hear her heartbeat pounding in her ears. She shakily stood up and took a deep breath, trying to steady herself. She squinted at the low setting sun in front of her. Ann heard a whinny behind her. She turned around just as Lucy's nose nuzzled her hand. "It's okay, girl," Ann said as she rubbed her hand up and down Lucy's blaze. She slowly walked back to the barn, laying one of her arms on Lucy's back.

As Ann finished up chores and headed back to the house, her feet felt heavy and her back ached. Her forehead was throbbing, and she stumbled over her gum boots several times before she finally got to the back door. She pulled her boots off and slipped into her room before her mom could see her forehead. She glanced in her vanity mirror to see a nice-sized welt forming. "Thank goodness Mom didn't see this . . . ," Ann said. "Maybe it will look better before suppertime." Her lack of sleep and her sore body slowly encouraged her to go lie in bed for just a little nap . . .

Chapter 7

Annabelle woke up to the sound of light rain. She stretched, then pulled the quilt tightly around her once more. She could hear Merry Anne working in the kitchen. Annabelle sighed and reluctantly pulled herself out of bed. She felt sore, and her head hurt.

"Good morning!" Merry Anne greeted Annabelle with a smile. "You're just in time for some tea and eggs."

As Merry Anne was pouring the tea, Whitney knocked and walked into the cottage. "Hello, ladies," Whitney said with a smile. Her long blonde hair was pulled back into a ponytail and she was once again wearing a pale-blue dress with a white apron. "Merry Anne fixed your dress, Annabelle. It turned out beautifully." She held out Annabelle's dress. Annabelle stood up and took it out of Whitney's hands. "My brother will be leaving for Pelland soon, if you would still like to catch a ride with him."

"Thank you both for how wonderful you have been to me," Annabelle said, smiling graciously. She held out her ruby-red dress; the stitching looked just perfect. "It looks amazing, I don't know when you even had time to do this," Annabelle said to Merry Anne. "I'll change, and then I'm ready to go." Annabelle quickly stepped out of the kitchen and back into the room she'd slept in. After changing and attempting to fold the apron and dress as nicely as she had received it, Annabelle took a deep breath and prepared herself for the trip back to Pelland. No matter how long of a ride it would be, it wouldn't be near long enough to prepare her for the earful Aunt Ester would be giving her for being gone.

Annabelle left the room and stopped by the kitchen to quickly eat the eggs and drink the tea Merry Anne had left on the table for her.

When Annabelle stepped outside, she took a moment to enjoy the rays of sun that were trying to pierce through the grey skies. The storm had ended. She met eyes with a very handsome man with curly brown hair who was leaning against the fence around the cottage entrance. He had vibrant blue eyes and a smile that made Annabelle's heart skip a beat. "Hello, Annabelle," the young man said in a deep, smooth voice. "I'm Nicholas, Whitney's older brother. Merry Anne and Whitney had to get to work, but they told me to wait outside for you."

Annabelle smiled. Travel would not be difficult with such a nice view, she thought to herself. "Thank you for being willing to take me to Pelland, Nicholas." As she attempted to gracefully glide down the few steps to be eye level with Nicholas, Annabelle slipped on the wet stone and stumbled awkwardly to the bottom step.

Nicholas caught Annabelle's hand. "Are you alright there, Miss Annabelle?" he asked with a chuckle. "And you can call me Nick."

"Yes, the step . . . it's a little slick," Annabelle said,

trying to hide her flushed cheeks behind her hair.

Nick walked Annabelle back to the stables where she'd left the beautiful black mare. They passed the little pond Annabelle saw when she first came into the town. Several large frogs hopped in the water as they walked by. Annabelle studied the houses. They were older than Pelland's cottages, and the roads were dirt, not cobblestone. It was an older town, known for its well-trained horses and blacksmiths.

Annabelle and Nick approached the small wooden wagon she had seen pull into the barn last night. A bored buckskin horse hitched up to the wagon was pawing at the dirt, anxious to get moving. Annabelle ran her fingers down the muzzle of the horse as it gave her a soft whinny in greeting. Nick helped Annabelle up into the wagon. She was very careful to pick up her dress and not snag it on anything. Nick climbed up beside her and grabbed the reins. The buckskin's ears perked forward, ready for action. With the click of Nick's tongue and a flick of the reins, they were off.

"Tell me about yourself, Nick," Annabelle said, glancing over at the handsome young man. "Have you always lived here?"

Nick smiled. "My family has roots in Emerson's Town deeper than some of the oldest trees. I love the town and enjoy the work. What about you, Annabelle? Has Pelland always been your home?"

"Yes, but I hope to see more of the world someday," she said, looking into his brilliant blue eyes. "Sometimes I just feel trapped." Annabelle was surprised at the boldness in her words. She had never said what she dreamed of out loud before. Her Aunt Ester would be shocked. She could just picture Aunt Ester now, with her arms folded as she gave the speech about how wonderful Pelland was, that there was no reason to want to be anywhere else. It didn't matter what Annabelle dreamed of when she lived within the castle walls. As the princess, her future—her *fate*—was already decided for her.

As they passed through the edge of town, Nick paused to say hello to two older women standing beside a weathered wooden produce-and-flower stand. With a smile and a wink, one of the women tossed Nick a daisy. He smiled as he handed it to Annabelle. "That would be my grandmother and her sister," he said as he waved goodbye to them.

Annabelle blushed as she held the flower in her hand. "Thank you."

Talking to Nick came easily. Soon they found themselves discussing their dreams of the future, personal interests, and hobbies. Nick talked about his passions of hunting and trapping. Annabelle shared about her love of art and her horses. They told stories of their families and friends. Annabelle intentionally left out the fact that her father was the king. She wasn't sure Nick would be comfortable talking so openly with the princess.

Nick handed Annabelle a sandwich. She didn't realize it was already past noon. "Merry Anne packed us lunch. Her spiced beef is amazing."

Annabelle looked at the sandwich Nick handed her. Her stomach growled with hunger. She took a bite, chewing quickly. "Thank you," she said, "it tastes delicious."

The time flew by, and before Annabelle realized it, they were riding through the woods that she and her umbrella had flown over the day before. Annabelle watched the trees move past them. Nick hummed a low tune while they rode. Annabelle closed her eyes and enjoyed the sound of the horse's hooves and Nick's tune.

"We are just about to Pelland. I need to stop in town to drop off a few things at our spot in the market, then we will get you home."

Annabelle opened her eyes and looked around. She hadn't even realized they had made it so close to town. Soon she'd be facing the wrath of one distraught Aunt Ester. Thoughts of her soft bed and warm quilt sounded wonderful.

The wagon passed by the boundary wall that bordered Pelland. The beautiful cottages and cobblestone roads were a welcoming sight. Annabelle watched as the townspeople went about their business. Gardeners were digging in one of the flowerbeds where the wind had ripped up the daffodils and scattered tree branches around the town.

Nick and Annabelle both laughed as they watched a group of small children chasing a loose chicken. Annabelle loved the buzz of the town. It was busy, and for the first time she felt like she could blend in. No one was staring at her as she and Nick rode by in the little wooden wagon. She had gone through the town completely unnoticed. Annabelle felt like she could be herself, laughing freely without worrying whether she would be assumed improper. She could talk to Nick without stirring up the town gossips, as they would twist anything they saw into trouble.

Nick pulled the wagon into the courtyard. It was full of carts and vendor stands. Nick inched the wagon through the crowd. "We are here," he said, pulling back the reins of the horse, bringing the wagon to an abrupt halt.

"Best if you stick by the wagon. After I get this delivered, I'll come back and drop you off at your house. Is it far from town?" Nick asked, pulling a burlap bag full of apples off the wagon.

"No, not far at all," Annabelle said. She didn't want him to know she lived in the castle of Pelland. But she wasn't sure how she was going to be able to hide who she was either. Now that they sat at the crowded market, there were a number of people staring in surprise at the sight of her. Aunt Ester didn't let her go to town very often, especially during the hustle and bustle of the farmer's market. Annabelle watched Nick walk off into the crowd. Just as she was losing sight of Nick, an old woman grabbed Annabelle's ankle. She looked down from the wagon in surprise.

"Annabelle?" the old woman asked. A black cloak covered her from head to toe. Just her wrinkled, weathered face and curly grey hair peaked through the hood.

"Yes?" Annabelle replied, fighting the urge to pull her ankle away.

"I am Raj, the town's fortune-teller. Come down and give me your hand."

Annabelle hesitated. Her Aunt Ester always told her to stay away from fortune-tellers. Aunt Ester's voice echoed in her head: "Always up to trouble they are, never EVER let them look into your future." She shrugged off Ester's voice and climbed down from the wagon.

Raj grinned as Annabelle held out her hand. The

fortune-teller took Annabelle's hand in her own twisted, wrinkled hands. Her nails were long and yellowed. "Let us see what life will have in store for you, little Princess." Raj's grey-green eyes glazed over and lost focus, as if she were really seeing what the future had in store for Annabelle.

"Annabelle!" Nick's voice called from the other side of the wagon. "Annabelle, get back into the wagon!"

Nick's voice snapped Annabelle's mind back from its reverie, and she pulled her hand out of the fortune-teller's. The fortune-teller's eyes cleared. "A traveler," the fortune-teller whispered in surprise as Nick grabbed Annabelle's arm and gently pulled her away from Raj. "Be alert, little Princess. Life has much in store for you. Two worlds are yours, but soon you will have to make a choice." And with that, the fortune-teller melted away, back into the crowd.

"Fortune-tellers are never up to any good, Annabelle. That's why I told you to stay by the wagon," Nick said, his deep-blue eyes looking into her own.

"Sorry, I guess I just wasn't thinking," Annabelle said, running what the fortune-teller said through her head once more. "Makes no sense at all," Annabelle thought to herself as she climbed back into the wagon beside Nick.

"Here, eat some supper," Nick said, handing Annabelle a jelly sandwich and an apple. "Sorry it isn't much."

"It's perfect, thank you," Annabelle said, taking a bite. She watched the colors of the sky change to oranges, pinks, and purples as the sun set. "Today has gone by so quickly. I wish I had more time to talk with you. I hope we see each other again."

Nick smiled. "Truly, it was a wonderful day. We'd best

get moving; it will be getting dark soon. I come to Pelland's market frequently. I could add your house to my visits if you would like."

"I would love that," Annabelle said, smiling.

Nick squeezed Annabelle's hand and then picked up the horse's reins. Her heart skipped a beat. His palm was rough and calloused. "Tell me, where are we going?"

Annabelle looked nervously at Nick's face. "I live in the castle."

Nick smiled. "I've only been close to it once; it is a beautiful place. They take great care of their staff, don't they?"

Annabelle nodded. "Yes, everyone is treated like family."

Slowly, Nick navigated the wagon out of the crowded market and down the hilly road toward the castle. The rolling pastures were beautiful at dusk. Annabelle's horses playfully chased the wagon.

The castle quickly came into view, towering over the tiny wagon. As they stopped in front of the entrance of the castle, Aunt Ester came running out. "Annabelle!" she shouted, her feet barely touching the steps as she ran down them. "I cannot believe this! Being gone so long and now showing up in a little rickety old wagon!"

Nick's eyes met Annabelle's and she smiled apologetically. "Aunt Ester . . . ," she called back. Annabelle hugged Nick, thanking him for the ride and stepping out of the wagon.

"To your room, Princess. Your father will be home tomorrow. He can deal with you then! Your hair is a disaster! And where are your shoes?! If your father were here, oh you would be in so much trouble!"

Annabelle looked back at Nick, his mouth open in surprise, still processing what was just said. "Thank you, Nick," Annabelle said, walking up the steps and into the castle.

Annabelle went into her room and opened her window, the one that started the whole adventure. She waved goodbye once more as Nick got his wagon turned around and headed down the road. She was sad to watch him leave. With a sigh she walked away from the window and got into her own bed. As happy as she was to be home, it was hard to say goodbye to Nick and to all the wonderful people she had met on her adventure.

As much as Annabelle tried, she couldn't fall asleep. Her mind was flooded by thoughts of the young Alec, who was working and missing school, and Whitney. . . . The world outside the castle was heartless.

A soft tapping came on Annabelle's window. She frowned and climbed out of bed. A shadow was cast on her windowsill. As Annabelle opened her window, she met the most beautiful blue eyes—Nick's. "Sorry to wake you, Annabelle, but I couldn't leave yet." He took Annabelle's hands in his own. "Not without . . ." And with that, Nick kissed her. His warm, soft lips made her heart flutter. As he pulled away, his eyes met hers. "We have a connection, I know it. I felt it on the ride to town and in the market. Princess or not, I hope we meet again."

Before Annabelle could even say a word, Nick silently climbed down from her rooftop and disappeared into the shadows. As she looked into the darkness, she tried to decide if she was dreaming. A long time passed before Annabelle realized she was clutching something in her hands. When she opened them, she found a braided twine bracelet. She knew Nick had made it, probably while he was waiting for darkness to fall and come back to her. Annabelle felt like she was soaring. She climbed back into bed with Nick's bracelet on her wrist and a smile on her face.

Chapter 8

Ann opened her eyes and climbed out of bed. She squinted; the light of the morning sun streaming through the windows made her head pound. Ann walked down her hallway, but the floor began to spin. She sat down on the antique mahogany bench and closed her eyes. When she opened them again, her eyes were looking right into her mother's, which were filled with concern. "Oh, Ann. What on earth happened?! You have a welt the size of a golf ball on your face!"

"You sure know how to make a girl feel better, Mom," Ann said, standing up. Her back and body hurt more than she remembered.

Ann's mom ran downstairs, opened the freezer, and made it back up the stairs before Ann could hear the click of the door shutting. "Here, I brought you an ice pack," Ann's mom said, pushing the ice pack against Ann's forehead.

"Burr!" Ann whined, pulling the ice pack off her forehead. As she pulled her hand back, her eyes caught sight of something new around her wrist, a little braided bracelet. Just like the one she had dreamed about. Ann caught her breath as she brought her arm closer to her face for a better look.

"You know, you aren't supposed to go to sleep when you get a head injury, Ann Jeanne," her mom said, frowning in concern. "When you came back in the house from doing chores, I figured you were tired, because you never came down for supper. I just let you sleep, but clearly I should have checked on you and made you wake up for supper."

"I'm sorry, Mom. . . . I fell off Lucy. My own fault . . . ," Ann trailed off, racking her brain for some reason how this could be real. "I really must have hit my head hard."

Ann's mom helped her down the stairs and into a chair at the kitchen table. "Let me heat up your dinner and then you can take a warm bath. You are a dusty mess."

Ann didn't even argue. She silently ate her warmed up dinner, chasing peas around her plate as she tried to wrap her mind around the possibilities of how this bracelet was really around her wrist, and not in her dreams. Her feet had been dirty—red dirt like the path she had walked along in her dreams, as well. But how could this be real?

"Ann, are you okay?" her mother asked, a concerned look in her eyes. "It seems like you have been different lately. Are you worried about going to college? We have talked about this; I will be fine on my own."

"No, Mom, it isn't that," Ann said, standing up and putting her plate in the sink. "I just am feeling a bit out of place, I guess you could say. Why didn't you ever date after Dad left, anyway?"

"Oh, Ann. . . . I always thought he would come back.

He still could. And if not, no one could ever fill his place."

Ann walked over to her mother and gave her a kiss on the top of her head. "I love you. I think I'm ready for that bath now."

A soak in the bathtub was what Ann needed; her head felt clearer. Ann tossed her clothes in the laundry basket in her room and then paused to twist the bracelet that was securely tied around her wrist a few times, as if she thought it might disappear.

"Feeling better?" Ann's mom asked, interrupting her train of thought.

"Yes, thank you, Mom," Ann said, smiling at her. "I need to run into town and pick up a textbook from school, and maybe see if my friends are around." Ann decided that some time with her friends might be a nice distraction, and she could use some fun.

"Sure, sweetie," her mom said. "But you won't be driving, not with that lovely welt. I would feel better if you let me drive you to town. I have some errands to run anyway."

"Deal," Ann said. "Let me go get ready."

It was afternoon by the time Ann and her mom headed out the door. Lucy whinnied when she saw them outside on the porch. She flicked her tail in excitement as Ann's mom's car got closer. Lucy chased them in the pasture as the car drove all the way down the lane. Ann waved goodbye to Lucy, smiling.

"I texted Noah, and he said he could give me a ride home. If you want to drop me off at Dirksen's Café, we can get some ice cream and then go to school together. I think Megan and Grace are meeting us there, too."

"Okay, just please text me when you're on your way

home," her mom said, turning onto the road that led to town. "I just want to make sure you're safe and feeling better."

"I'm already feeling better."

When they pulled into a parking spot in front of the café, Ann unbuckled her seatbelt, reached over and put her hand on her mom's. "I love you; I'll text you later."

"Thank you. I love you, too," Ann's mom said as Ann climbed out of the car. She waved goodbye as her mom pulled back into the street.

Megan was already seated inside when Ann walked in. She smiled as Ann sat down beside her. "Did you head-butt a cement wall, Ann? That looks pretty rough."

Ann laughed, "Yeah, I thought it would make me look tougher, as if school finals wouldn't beat me up enough."

Noah and Grace squished into the booth, sitting across from Megan and Ann. "I'm glad you thought of this, Ann," Grace said. "Ice cream sounds tasty, but you might need some to put on your face today."

"Man, my friends sure know how to make me feel better," Ann said, laughing while she playfully scowled at them.

The group ordered their ice cream to go, and then piled into Noah's blue truck to head to school. "Ice cream will make having to go to school better," Noah said, shutting the truck door.

The drive to school was short, and the group spent most of it laughing and trying to eat their melting ice cream. Ann loved the time spent with her friends; they always knew how to make her forget about her troubles. She had a hard time imagining what life will be like when they all went off to different colleges. She was going to miss them dearly.

The group made their trip to the school brief, getting the textbook Ann needed and dropping off Grace's and Megan's science project. When they piled back into Noah's truck, Ann felt tired again.

"Do you guys want to come over to my house?" Noah asked, pulling the truck out of the parking lot. "It would be a fun day to ride four-wheelers."

"Yes!" Grace and Megan said.

"I probably should head home, I'm feeling pretty tired," Ann said. "Sorry to be a party pooper."

"No problem, Ann," Noah said. "With a welt like that, you probably are pretty worn out."

The sun was setting when Noah pulled into Ann's driveway. Ann climbed out and waved goodbye to her friends as she watched them drive back down her lane. She was happy to be home, but sad to miss out on more fun with them.

"Hey, sweetie," Ann's mom called from the porch. "Come enjoy some peppermint tea with me."

Ann climbed onto the porch and sat in the rocking chair beside her mom. The crickets and frogs started to sing, and soon a group of deer had come out to graze in the field in front of the house.

"Let's get some dinner," Ann's mom said, standing up from her chair.

"That sounds good," Ann replied. The deer paused to look up and watch Ann and her mom go inside the house.

"Tacos?" Ann asked, pulling a pound of hamburger from the fridge.

"Tacos," her mom said, handing Ann a skillet.

They shared stories about their day while they cooked

and then ate dinner. "You had better get some studying in before bed," Ann's mom said, picking up their plates. "I can take care of the dishes."

"Thanks, Mom," Ann said, scooting her chair in and then heading upstairs.

The evening went by quickly, and Ann got more homework done than she thought she would. When her alarm clock blinked to 9:30 PM, she stifled a yawn and shut her textbook. "Time for bed," she told Cleo as she pushed her backpack off her bed.

Ann turned her light off, climbed into bed, and hugged her pillow to her chest. Her hand touched the bracelet she was wearing, and her mind started racing again. If she dreamed about the same place over and over again, what would that mean? How is it even possible that she had this bracelet? She turned the bracelet around and around until the twine burned her wrist. Soon she drifted off to sleep.

Chapter 9

Annabelle woke up as the sun streamed into her windows and chased away the shadows of night. She arched her back and stretched. Before opening her eyes, her mind played through the events of the past few days: a wonderful adventure, a first kiss, and a bracelet from a handsome young man. She opened her eyes and pulled her arm out from under her quilts to look at the bracelet. As she studied the curves of the twine her eyes caught the slight rope burn that was around her wrist.

She sat straight up in bed. Was this real? Annabelle shook her head. How would that be possible? She studied the rope burn once more. How could her dreams of a different world, of the red pickup truck and her mother, be more than just dreams? She thought of her mother. All the times she wondered what her real mother looked like or wishing to spend time with her. When Annabelle kept thinking her dreams were just dreams, she was truly seeing her real mother. Annabelle closed her eyes and pictured her mother's face. So many questions flooded into her head. Somehow, some way, she was living in two different places at the same time. Annabelle laughed out loud. She must be going crazy. Suddenly she remembered what the fortune-teller at the market had told her. Raj was right. A *traveler*. Of course! Impossible!

Annabelle quickly climbed out of bed and got dressed. Her father would be coming home today; she knew she could confide in him. A knock on her bedroom door interrupted her thoughts. "Annabelle, come down and have something to eat," Aunt Ester called from the other side of the door.

"Yes, Aunt Ester," Annabelle said, pulling a comb through her dark brown hair and opening her door.

Aunt Ester met Annabelle with a smile. Her tired grey eyes searched Annabelle's face. "Is everything okay?" Aunt Ester asked, raising her eyebrows as she touched her thin, bony hand to Annabelle's cheek.

"Yes, just fine," Annabelle lied, walking past Aunt Ester and heading down to get some breakfast. "I'm just ready to see my father."

Shortly after eating, Annabelle walked outside and untangled her swing from the old oak tree. She tucked in her olive-green dress, sat on the wooden seat, and kicked her shoes off. Annabelle dug her toes in the dirt and slowly pushed herself back and forth. The morning breeze was cool and crisp, rustling the leaves of the trees as it blew through their branches. The birds were calling merrily to each other from the surrounding trees. The castle grounds were buzzing with work all around her. The gardeners were pulling fresh carrots from the rich black dirt and piling them into wicker baskets. Her horses were trotting to the barn from the rolling pastures for their breakfast of oats and hay, the pounding of their hooves echoing through the hills.

The sound of wagon wheels silenced the singing birds. Annabelle dug her heels into the dirt to slow her swinging. As the wagon rolled to a stop next to the tree, Annabelle stood up from the old swing and jumped into her dad's open arms. She breathed in the scent of worn leather and sweat. "Welcome home!" Annabelle said, leaning back in his arms to look at him.

Annabelle closely resembled her father. They shared the same sharp green eyes and dark, chestnut-colored hair, although more grey had crept into his hair and beard since she had seen him last. A smile lit up his face. "It is so good to see you, my dear," he said, hugging her tightly.

"Did you find what you were looking for?" Annabelle asked.

She could feel her father's chest sink as he slowly exhaled. "No. But this was the last trip. . . . I. . . . I don't have any other resources," he said. "Your Aunt Ester wants me to focus on other things, and she's right. I just wasn't ready to give up yet."

Annabelle was silent for a moment and then asked, "What have you been searching for?" He took her arm in his as they walked into the castle. "You have spent years on this, and how many months you have spent away from me? I am old enough to know."

"You're right, Annabelle. After dinner tonight, I—"

"James!" Aunt Ester called as she ran up to embrace her brother, cutting his talk with Annabelle short. "You are finally home safe." Ester took her brother's hand and led him out of the foyer and down the hall, leaving Annabelle behind.

Annabelle stayed back and bit her cheek in frustration.

There is never enough time with him; if it isn't Aunt Ester, it's his duties as king or whatever it was that he was searching for.

"Annabelle, do not forget your studies!" Aunt Ester called from down the hall. "You must meet with Kristina at her cottage in the meadow. You are falling behind, and what kind of prince would want a future queen that lacks necessary education? The clock is ticking to find you a suitor!"

"Yes, Aunt Ester," Annabelle said, rolling her eyes.

Annabelle walked back outside and headed toward the cottage near the meadow. She stopped by the oak tree to scratch behind the ears of her black-and-white spotted rat terrier, Rosie, who was laying on her stomach in the grass soaking up the sun. Rosie's ears perked forward, and she quickly jumped up and trotted in front of Annabelle, looking back frequently to ensure Annabelle was still there, her little docked tail wriggling with pride as she led the way to the cottage.

"Kristina?" Annabelle called as she stepped into the cottage.

"Good morning," Kristina called back as she met Annabelle with a stack of books. She cradled the books in one arm and used her other hand to tuck a strand of her rich brown hair behind her ear. Kristina's skin was a beautiful brown, tan from hours spent in the sun. She was very thin and elegant. Frequently Annabelle would find herself wishing to have the grace that Kristina was blessed with.

The morning passed slowly for Annabelle, her mind wandering back to her recent discovery of living in two worlds. She wondered what her father was searching for, and what he would think when she told him about recent events. By the time her lesson was done, the sun was setting. Annabelle picked up a few of the books off the table, and woke Rosie, who was soundly sleeping under a chair in the study. Rosie yawned, stretched, and led Annabelle back to the castle.

The castle yard was full of people, excited to celebrate the king's return. "Annabelle!" a familiar voice called. She looked up to see Nick, just as handsome as she remembered, and Whitney, walking toward her and waving.

"What are you guys doing here?" Annabelle asked in surprise.

"We heard your father came home, and the castle was in need of extra hands for all the horses here. Whitney and I volunteered to come help," Nick replied, bending down to pet Rosie, who was intensely sniffing Nick's boots.

"You really are the princess from Pelland!" Whitney exclaimed. "I am so sorry we didn't realize it." Whitney's golden-blonde hair was pulled back into a braid. She was wearing a pale-blue dress, similar to what Annabelle had seen her in before.

Annabelle grinned. "The condition I was in when you saw me, I would not have believed it myself! It is so good to see you again." Annabelle's eyes met Nick's. "I have been thinking about you."

"Annabelle!" Aunt Ester's voice rang out into the yard. "Enough fraternizing with the help. You need to get cleaned up for the dinner party!"

"Yes, Aunt Ester," Annabelle replied flatly. "It was so good to see both of you." Annabelle put her hands on both

Whitney and Nick in parting as she walked back to the castle.

Dinner was frustrating. Annabelle chased peas around her plate with her silverware as she half-listened to the conversation around her. The table was filled with people she barely knew. She wished she had Nick and Whitney to talk to, or just had some time to talk with her father before this whole thing. Her mind wandered to Merry Anne, Emerson's Town, and the people she had met. Annabelle felt like her father was still far away, even though he was sitting beside her. She had so many things she wanted to ask him. Slowly the crowd thinned until it was just Aunt Ester and her father sitting beside her at the table. "Ester, I would like some time to talk with Annabelle," her father said, standing up from his chair. "I will talk with you tomorrow."

"But James, it is late enough as it is. Don't you need some sleep?" Aunt Ester asked, raising her eyebrows and pursing her lips into a thin line.

"I will be just fine, Ester," Annabelle's father said, taking Annabelle's hand and leading her out of the dining hall, through the foyer, and out of the castle. "Let's go to the stables. It will be quiet there; we will be able to talk." He led Annabelle into the stables in silence; only the sound of Rosie panting filled the air as she pushed her pudgy little body to keep up, following closely at their heels.

Annabelle sat on a hay bale resting against the wooden fence. Her father sat beside her, her hand resting loosely in his. Rosie sat on Annabelle's feet, gazing up at them, her ears cocked forward in curiosity.

Her father smiled a sad smile, sighed, and said, "Okay,

my dear. Here is the story." He paused for a long time, almost making Annabelle think he wasn't going to share. Eventually, he continued: "There is so much mystery in life. Aunt Ester and I have kept you tucked away from parts of the outside world. The peasants, the fortune-tellers, Gypsies, nomads, adventure, magic . . ." He paused to study Annabelle's face. She was listening patiently.

"This may be hard to believe or even understand. But I am going to try and share it with you. Our family is not typical . . . and it isn't just because we are royalty. There is magic in our blood. Some of us are blessed with the ability to travel. And it isn't just travel from town to town. Some of us can travel through different worlds. . . . I am sure this is hard to comprehend. The people in our family who have enough magic running through them can share the two worlds and have a life in each one. As we jump between the two parallel worlds, we have no idea how much time will have lapsed. What seems like hours may be minutes, what seems like a day may be hours. It's difficult to understand—but it always seems to happen as one goes to sleep.

"Most travelers only travel with their mind, not their body, so it isn't even noticeable that they are gone. Sometimes their lives can happen without even being aware they have two lives; one life feels like a dream. They can live like this their entire life, not aware that they are traveling.

"However, there are rare ones with more magic who are able to remember both worlds and become aware of their ability. Once the person becomes aware of the two lives, that person's two bodies become one and are no longer allowed to live in both worlds. These people travel between the two worlds and only have a certain amount of time to pick one before their ability to travel in between the two ends. There is no set time for the ability to end. It could be days, it could be weeks, or even months. But once it happens, you're permanently in the world you picked. The belief is that travelers are able to know when their last trip will be.

"I once was able to travel between two worlds. The life I lived parallel to this one is very far away, and very different. You have a life there that mixed with mine that you are not even aware of. In that life, I was married to an amazing woman, your mother. When you were born, I began to dream of you in this world as well. This means the magic runs in your veins, just like me. But your mother is not here because she doesn't carry the magic. Because your mother doesn't have magic in her veins, you will never be able to connect your worlds or fully travel, and you won't have to worry about picking a world.

"My worlds connected, I became aware of both lives, and time ran out for me. I wanted to stay in that life, with your mother and with you. I thought I knew when my last trip would be. I picked the world with you and your mother—or at least I thought I did. I guess fate had other plans for me, and I lost her." Her father blinked back tears as he squeezed Annabelle's hand.

"When I was in the world your mother is in, I was working in the military, helping to keep our country safe. In Pelland, I applied my knowledge to help the townspeople not only in this city but also in our entire kingdom. Trolls were waging war on Emerson's Town. They had come from the Enchanted Forest, destroying everything in their path. I used my experience to lead the fight and save the town and people. The king died in battle, but his last request was for me to carry on the work for our town. Soon after that, the people of the kingdom entrusted me to become king. I gained the respect of the villages and towns. During this time, I lost the ability to travel between the two worlds. I have helped really grow Pelland and protect people in need, but I have missed your mother and think of her every day. Losing her weighs heavily on my heart. That is why I have been looking for a way back to her.

"I know it sounds crazy; I have kept you too sheltered from the outside world. I should have let you come with me to meet the witches and wizards, the Gypsies and fortune-tellers. I should have shown you the Mysterious Island and walked you through the Enchanted Forest. I should have told you more about your mother and the traveling. Aunt Ester could travel too, but that is her story to tell. You have grown so quickly, and when I realized how much I hid from you, you were already a young woman. I am so sorry, my dear Annabelle." His voice wavered, sounding full of remorse and sorrow.

After a moment of silence, Annabelle spoke: "I have not missed out on all the adventures life has to offer."

Her father raised one eyebrow and replied, "Please explain."

Annabelle proceeded to tell him about her trip to Emerson's Town, what Raj the fortune-teller had told her, but didn't mention her kiss with Nick. She told him of her life with her mom, every detail down to her beat-up old pickup truck.

He laughed and clapped his hands together. "All this time, Annabelle!" He stood up and put his hands on her shoulders. He looked so full of hope, a smile filling his face. "I have been out searching for other travelers, but they are a dying breed, one until now I thought was extinct. As they mix with people who do not travel and have children, the ability to travel dies out; our family is close to the last to be able to do it. I knew you were in this life, and with me in the other world, but again, because you didn't get magic from your mother, I never dreamed you would connect your two worlds or be able to fully travel between them! I have been meeting with some witches and wizards in hopes they could create a potion to bring me back to your mother, but to no avail." His smile fell from his face; his hands dropped from Annabelle's shoulders to his sides. "How long have you been able to do this? We don't know how much time you have, your mother must already feel abandoned by me, and she cannot lose you, too!" A look of worry now covered her father's face as he sat down beside Annabelle again.

"It hasn't been long, maybe a week," Annabelle replied. "So, this means. . . . I am going to lose you or mom?"

"Yes," her father replied, taking her hand in his. "I beg you to pick your mother. She doesn't know about the traveling. When I discovered what was happening to me, we would go to sleep in bed together only for her to wake up without me. I would come back to her world and she would find me back in bed. I had no explanation of what happened. She knew something wasn't right, but I never could find it in me to tell her—she would have thought I was a lunatic!"

Annabelle chewed on one of her fingernails, a habit her Aunt Ester had been trying to break her of. "There has to be another way." She thought of all her friends in her other world, her mother, her home, and then her mind wandered to what adventures she could have here with her father, and what friendships she could make. It seemed like just recently she had been able to discover herself here.

They sat in silence for a while. Her father yawned and rubbed his face with his hands. "It's best we get you to bed, princess. We can talk more tomorrow." He stood up and helped Annabelle to her feet. Her mind was almost numb, overloaded with so much to comprehend. When they reached the stairs to her room, he gave her a hug. "Safe travels tonight. Please hug your mother for me."

Annabelle stumbled to the top of the steps. She walked into her room, sat on the edge of her bed, and tucked her knees to her chest. Tears ran down her cheeks. Today at dawn she felt that so many doors had opened, and by dusk the walls were closing in. Her thoughts were interrupted as her bedroom door opened. Aunt Ester was standing in the doorway. Her silvery-grey hair was piled in a bun on top of her head; she was draped in a mink fur shawl. Aunt Ester always seemed so strong and refined, but tonight she looked withered and resigned. "James told me he shared his story with you, and that now you must make a big decision." She paused a minute as she sank beside Annabelle on the bed. "I had a feeling the day would come that this would happen to you. You have too much of your father in you to not be a true traveler, too. I have thought a lot about what you would decide, your life in the world with your mother or your life here. But. . . . What if you could keep both, forever?"

Annabelle sat up straight, swinging her feet off the

bed to the floor. "What do you mean?"

Aunt Ester took Annabelle's hand in hers. "I know of a witch in the Enchanted Forest. She has worked with travelers for centuries. She can't revive the power to travel, but I believe she can keep it going."

Annabelle exhaled, not even realizing she had been holding her breath. "How do I find her? Does my father know about her?" Annabelle's eyes glimmered with hope in the light of the lantern that Aunt Ester held.

"She is well known in the kingdom, but she is hard to find. She moves around a lot. Your father went to meet her once, but he was seeking someone to bring his ability to travel back, not to extend it. I will talk with him tomorrow to get a group together to go with you on this journey. It will be your first adventure. . . . It's time to get your feet wet."

"Thank you, Aunt Ester," Annabelle said in surprise. Aunt Ester had always been so overprotective, Annabelle never expected her to help.

Aunt Ester smiled, kissed Annabelle on the forehead, and then left, shutting the door behind her. Annabelle curled up in her bed and closed her eyes. Even though it had just been one day, it felt like a lifetime since she had seen her mother.

Chapter 10

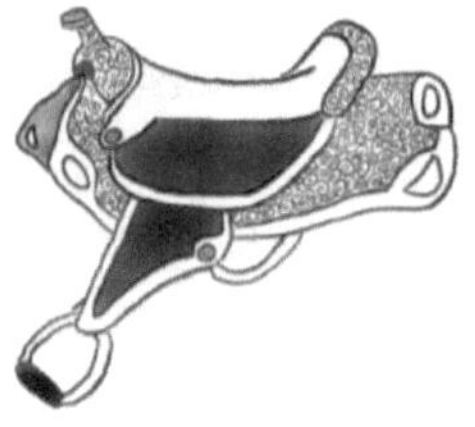

The alarm buzzed loudly in Ann's room. She reached over and shut it off without opening her eyes. She lay in bed and listened to the world around her. She could hear dishes clanking together in the sink as her mother washed them. She heard the patter of her cat, Cleo's, feet as she jumped on Ann's bed and climbed over the blankets to rest on her chest. Ann smiled and dug her fingers into Cleo's long, soft, gray fur. Cleo purred in contentment.

Ann moved Cleo off her chest and climbed out of bed. She headed toward the hallway, stopping to look back and smile at Cleo, whose bright yellow eyes were scowling when Ann stopped petting her.

Ann's mother was still in the kitchen, drying off her hands with a towel, when Ann got downstairs. She gave her a loving hug, breathing in her comforting fragrance, like lilacs. Ann couldn't imagine her life without her mom.

"Good morning, sweetie," Ann's mom said, hugging her back and kissing her on the top of her head. "I hope you got some restful sleep last night. I made cinnamon rolls for breakfast, and if you don't have too much homework to do maybe we could take Lucy on a few trail rides. The last time Sheila came over she said that Lucy was packing on too many pounds. We probably should get her out of the barn for a while."

Ann grinned. She loved riding horses with her mom. She knew Lucy had gained some weight. She was the most food-driven horse they had ever had. Whenever their vet, Sheila, would come over she would have a few carrots in her pocket just for Lucy. Sheila was one of the most trusted vets around, and one of Ann's mom's closest friends. "That sounds like a great plan." They finished breakfast and then Ann changed to go to the barn.

Ann and her mom were greeted by Lucy's deep whinny. There were days when Ann thought Lucy was more of a dog than a horse. She would insist on giving kisses to whomever entered the barn and would be at Ann's heels wherever she could follow her. Lucy would come running to her when Ann called her name.

Horses were just one of the many ways Ann and her mom spent time together. When Lucy was about a year old, Ann and her mom were working with Lucy in the front yard. Ann's mom bet Ann that Lucy wouldn't follow her into their house. Sure enough, Lucy happily followed Ann into their living room. She curiously sniffed the couch and looked around. When Ann would tell the story, friends would say their mothers wouldn't have allowed that.

Ann's mom was very supportive of Ann. She worked a full-time job and still made it to every extracurricular event Ann was in. If her mom wasn't working, she and Ann would work outside in the garden. Her mom had the greenest thumb, and Ann knew the name of almost every flower growing on their acreage thanks to her. Ann's mom never complained about not having time for herself or let Ann know about any worries she was carrying. For someone doing the work of two parents, Ann was very proud to have her.

The day flew by as Ann and her mom took turns riding Lucy while the other walked along beside. They talked about everything, from Ann's future plans to dating. Ann felt so blessed to have such a beautiful place to ride. She remembered how her dad carefully plotted the horse trails through their family's acreage for her mom, who had always had a passion for horses. He would routinely go out and cut back tree branches and mow the grass, so the trails were beautifully maintained for her. They walked past the barn her dad had built with his own two hands for Ann's mom. Ann thought about how much dedication and commitment he showed her mom—no wonder her mom thought he was going to come back some day.

They made their way back to the barn and unsaddled Lucy. Lucy's maple-brown hair was slimy with sweat. Ann rubbed Lucy's white blaze that stretched from her forehead to the tip of her nose. She watched as her mom gave Lucy some more oats and a scratch behind the ears. Her mom still had a youthful look about her, and unlike Ann and her dad, she had deep hazel-brown eyes. Ann's mom had always been strong and independent. She single-handedly kept the house in order, their finances, and provided for Ann's needs. She never showed signs of weakness, even when she would sit in the rocking chair on the front porch and look down the lane in the evenings. Ann knew her mom was hoping that one day she would see her dad coming home, but she would just tell Ann she liked to wait for the sun to set.

"Let's order pizza for dinner," Ann's mom said, shutting the barn gate and putting her arm around Ann's shoulders. "I don't care to cook, and I think there's a pretty good chick flick on the television tonight."

"Sounds perfect," Ann said, "I am starved!"

After dinner they curled up in blankets on the couch and watched their movie. When it was over, Ann stretched and yawned. She was so thankful to get to spend time with her mom. The day had worn her out. "I'm going to study and head to bed," Ann said, picking up her backpack in the hall.

"Okay, sweetie," Ann's mom said, giving her a hug good night. "Today was a good day."

"It really was, Mom," Ann said, walking up the stairs to her room. She could feel her tears burning in her eyes. "What if the days here are limited? What if I don't know when my time is up to travel and Mom is left alone? Who will take care of Mom then?" she thought to herself.

Ann shut the door to her room and laid her bag on the floor beside her bed. Who could study at a time like this? She didn't even know if she would be in this world to take her finals. Her head was spinning with worry and flooded with thoughts. She slowly drifted off to sleep.

Chapter 11

As the light streamed into Annabelle's room, she opened her eyes. Rosie was lying beside her bed, her chin resting on her crossed black-and-white-speckled front legs. "Hello, Rosie," Annabelle whispered. Rosie jumped to attention, her little tail wagging in anticipation. Annabelle swung her legs over the side of the bed and rubbed behind Rosie's big, black ears. "Time for a big day!" Annabelle said, and she was out of bed, dressed and heading down the stairs before Rosie even realized Annabelle was done petting her.

When Annabelle got to the foyer, she overheard Aunt Ester and her father talking heatedly. She slowed her walk to listen in, but her father caught sight of her. "Annabelle," he said, "we were just talking about you. Ester has asked me to consider you going on a journey. I have a meeting with Emerson. There are a lot of people in his town that could help you on your journey, many of them that went with me." Her father paused for a moment and then said, "I have sent word to Emerson to gather a group. This is going to be hard for me. I have spent so long trying to keep you safe. But Ester is right; you need to find your own way. After we get to Emerson's Town, I will pair you with a family I know there and let you go." Her father looked anxious. Annabelle knew this was going to be hard for him.

"Thank you. I will be careful, and I will come back," Annabelle said, her heart filling with hope. She ran back up the stairs and called behind her, "I will go pack a few things, and then I will be ready!"

Annabelle met her father outside the castle with a small pack on her shoulder. A carriage was waiting for them, pulled by two of their midnight-black draft horses. They pawed at the ground, anxiously waiting to get going. Aunt Ester put her hand on Annabelle's shoulder and lightly squeezed it. "Be safe," she said, giving Annabelle a nervous look.

"I will, Aunt Ester. Thank you for talking my father into this," Annabelle said, climbing into the carriage. She hoped that the trip to the town would go quickly; she had so much to get done and not enough time to do it. Her stomach was in knots.

On the ride Annabelle and her father talked about her day with her mother. She told him about how every evening her mother sits on the porch, waiting for him to come home. Her father swallowed hard. He didn't say anything; Annabelle could tell he was trying to fight the feelings of guilt and sadness.

Their carriage came to an abrupt stop. Her father stuck his head out the window of the carriage to see what was going on.

"Sorry, King James. Annabelle's dog has been

following us since we left the castle. We are far enough away now, she might not find her way back if we leave her," Will, the driver, called from the front.

Annabelle grinned. She climbed out of the carriage and scooped Rosie up in her arms. Rosie was panting hard. Annabelle looked into Rosie's big brown eyes with a scolding look. Rosie put her ears back in submission; she knew she shouldn't have followed the carriage, but she didn't want to miss out on the adventure! Rosie slept comfortably on Annabelle's lap the rest of the trip.

When the carriage rolled to a stop in Emerson's Town, a knot was forming in the pit of Annabelle's stomach. She was anxious to be back to where the wind had blown her, where she met Nick and so many other interesting people. She hoped she would see them again. "Will you keep Rosie here? I don't want her to get lost," Annabelle asked, laying the sleeping dog on the cushioned red velvet seat of the carriage.

"Yes, sweetie," her father said. "We shall leave her with Will until I'm done meeting with Emerson. He can keep an eye on her." Her father tied a rope around Rosie's neck and tied the other end to the door of the carriage. "That should keep the mutt for now," he said with a smile, climbing out of the carriage. "I sent for someone to help you get a group together, one of Emerson's men. He should be here shortly. For now, we could look around the market."

Annabelle was happy to walk around and spend time with her father. The market was bustling with people, packed shoulder to shoulder, slowly moving from vendor to vendor, almost like a water's current.

The vendor stands were small, crammed side by side

in tight rows. In order to provide the vendors and shoppers some relief from the sun, colorful canvas tarps had been tied to tall wooden posts that separated each stand. Annabelle felt overwhelmed by the commotion. The smell of the variety of food cooking made her mouth water. The noise of the crowd and vendors made her head hurt. There wasn't a tree in sight, and the ground had been stomped down by so much foot traffic that grass no longer tried to grow. When the wind blew, the dust would swallow the crowds of the market.

There was almost a halo around Annabelle and her father as the villagers gave them plenty of space. Annabelle could hear the whispers of "It's the king!" and "Is that really the princess, out of the castle?!" She never cared to be the center of attention but was happy she didn't feel crushed in the crowd. She paused at a vendor's table to look at wind chimes. The sun caught the colored glass and various pieces of metal. Annabelle reached up to touch it, making it clink and dance in the air. She looked up from the wind chime to see the vendor, a young boy, probably no older than ten, staring at her. She quickly broke eye contact and continued to look around the market. It had everything anyone could ever need, from produce to jewelry to goats and other livestock.

"King James!" a voice called. Her father stopped walking and scanned the crowd. He smiled and waved as a tall man in a brown leather jacket and forest-green pants came jogging up to meet them.

"Hello, Jesse!" her father called, as he reached out and shook Jesse's hand firmly. "It is so good to see you. We were just finishing up at the market, you have impeccable timing."

Jesse grinned. "It is good to see you, too. I was surprised to hear you needed me for another trip, when you have barely just gotten home."

"It is actually not for me," he replied, putting his hand on Annabelle's shoulder. "Annabelle is in need of some help." He paused for a minute, looking around at the crowd. "She can tell you about it at Emerson's; we have quite a few spectators here. Jesse, I don't expect you to go along. You need time to focus on the farm and your mother; just make sure she is in good hands." He turned to Annabelle: "Please be safe, sweetie. I have a few things to do here before I go to Emerson's; Jesse will take you there now. We don't have time to waste."

"Thank you, Father. I will see you soon," Annabelle said, hugging him goodbye. She tried to put on a brave face, giving her dad a reassuring smile as she walked away, only looking back twice. She followed Jesse to a white barn on the edge of the market where two horses were tied; they were charcoal colored with black-and-white tails. She swallowed the lump in her throat. She thought she was ready for an adventure, but the further she got from home, the more scared she felt.

Jesse turned around and leaned in toward her, making sure no one else would hear. "Don't be nervous, Princess. You will be home before you know it." He untied the horse's reins from the post and handed Annabelle one. "It isn't a long ride to Emerson's."

"He wouldn't believe I already know where Emerson's mansion is," Annabelle thought to herself, smiling and taking the reins from Jesse. Just as she was getting ready to climb on, she heard a dog's bark coming from the crowd. She paused, listening for it again. Another bark came, this time closer. It sounded familiar to Annabelle.

"Is everything okay?" Jesse asked, already on his horse.

"Yes, I—" Annabelle stopped mid-sentence as she caught a glimpse of Rosie, frantically running toward Annabelle, her black ears flopping in the wind. The rope her dad had used to keep her in the carriage was still tied around her neck; the other end was trailing behind her, bouncing along the dusty ground as she ran. "I guess I have one more joining the group," Annabelle said, scooping Rosie up in her arms. As silly as it was for Rosie to come along, it was comforting for Annabelle to hold her.

They arrived at the mansion just as the sun was beginning to set. Annabelle was excited to see Whitney again, and maybe she could get a chance to see Nick, too. She looked down at the bracelet Nick had given her. Her heart skipped a beat thinking of the kiss he had given her from her bedroom window.

"Annabelle!" Her thoughts were cut short. She looked up to see Merry Anne. "It is so good to see you! Jesse said he was meeting you and your father at the market today. I was happy to hear I was going to see you again."

Annabelle hadn't made the connection that Jesse was Merry Anne's son. She was so happy to see a familiar face. "It is so good to see you, Merry Anne!" Annabelle said, climbing off the horse. Rosie sniffed the hem of Merry Anne's skirt, perking her ears up in interest. "And this is Rosie; she is a tagalong for the trip."

Merry Anne bent down to tell Rosie hello. Rosie wagged her little docked tail as Merry Anne scratched her back. "Emerson is excited to meet you. He has heard a lot about you from your father."

"Let's go, I'm sure you will want to get settled in and cleaned up before dinner," Jesse said, leading Annabelle to Emerson's house. It was almost a castle, beautifully built and landscaped. Jesse showed her to the room she would be staying in for the night. "We will start our journey tomorrow. I'm sure after your trip today you are pretty tired; it's best to start fresh. I will have someone come for you when it is time for dinner. The rest of the group will be arriving soon, too."

Jesse left, shutting the door behind him and leaving Annabelle alone with Rosie in the room. Rosie sniffed around the parameter of the room, and then settled in beside the olive-colored canvas trunk at the end of the bed with a sigh. It wasn't long before she was sound asleep.

Annabelle washed her hands and face in the water basin that was in the room. She looked through the pack she had quickly thrown together: a few light cotton dresses, some fruit and spiced jerky, and a small knife her father had given her. She repacked it and set the pack beside the bed.

It wasn't long until she heard a knock at her door. "Dinner is ready, Princess."

Annabelle grinned; she knew that voice! She jumped off the bed and opened the door. She met Nick's handsome blue eyes. He was smiling from ear to ear.

"Nick!" Annabelle exclaimed, quickly wishing she had hidden some of her excitement. "What are you doing here?"

"I am part of the traveling party, so you will have to put up with me for the journey." He held out his arm for her to take. "Are you ready for dinner? It's time to meet the rest of the group." He was dressed in a nice button-down blue shirt and khaki-colored trousers. His brown curly hair was neatly combed.

"Yes!" Annabelle said, allowing him to lead her to the dining room. The table was full of people. The chatter stopped as they walked into the room. Annabelle's stomach turned. She knew all eyes were on her.

A short, chubby man stood up from the table. "Annabelle!" he announced. "It is so good to meet you! I am Emerson." He walked over and took one of Annabelle's hands in both of his. "I am honored that your father entrusted me to help you with this. We have been happily helping him on his journeys for years. As the mayor of this town, I can promise that your secret is safe with the traveling party, as it was with your father's missions. James told me what was going on, and said I could share with this group, and we are all so happy to serve your father, and now you. Come, sit and eat. I will introduce you."

He led Annabelle to the empty chair at the head of the table. Nick sat a few chairs down in the next empty seat. She had hoped he would be closer; in a group of strangers, it would be nice to have one familiar face for support. "I have selected a few strong individuals to go with you," Emerson said as he gestured to the man sitting on the other side of Annabelle. He had black hair, a crooked nose and a strong jaw line. He was very sturdily built. "This is Russell. He will serve as a guard for you." Russell nodded in acknowledgment. "The man sitting beside him is Gary, another guard. Gary is one of your father's special knights. He has saved your father's life on many occasions." Gary was leanly built with sandy-colored hair and grey-blue eyes. He smiled politely at Annabelle. "I don't expect there to be any troubles on this trip, but you never know what to expect with the Enchanted Forest. You should always plan for surprises." Emerson paused for a moment and took a drink of wine.

"We also need a tracker to find the witch you seek. We have many in my town, but there are only a select few who can track witches. Typically, Jesse is the one that we send with your father," he said, gesturing toward Jesse, who was sitting beside Gary. Annabelle hadn't even realized he was there. "But Jesse has just returned from a trip with your father, and I need him here. I am sending his mother, Merry Anne."

Annabelle smiled. She was very pleased to hear that Merry Anne would be joining her on the journey!

Emerson continued, "Merry Anne is very skilled, and has trained a lot of trackers. She has recently handed the task off to her son, Jesse, but was happy to accept my request for her to go with you. She is the best of the best; I have never had anyone better. Unfortunately, she didn't have time to come to dinner tonight; she is preparing for tomorrow."

Emerson took another bite of his dinner and then continued. "Lastly, I have asked Nicholas to go. He is one of my strongest hunters and trappers. You won't go hungry with him. He works with my animals and is very knowledgeable about plants and natural medicines. The rest of this group is just here to pack and prep; they won't be coming along."

Annabelle put her fork down and nervously cleared her throat. "Thank you all for being willing to accompany me on this journey. My family and I are deeply indebted to each of you for leaving your homes and families to come with me. The success of this journey is riding on our shoulders, and we will not fail."

"We would all follow King James to the end, Annabelle. It will be the same for you. Your family line is full of great leaders. Your father has saved this town on several occasions. We'll never forget how he led us to victory when the trolls invaded, or how he made sure every last cottage had food and water during past droughts. We will never be able to fully repay him, but we will do our best," Emerson said, patting her shoulder with his hand that he was holding his turkey leg in.

The rest of dinner was full of laughter and stories of old adventures. An old man with a long, silver beard sitting beside Nick shared a story about a trip with Annabelle's father to the Mysterious Islands. The entire crew got seasick, their food supply got wet and molded, and after they made it to the island, a witch turned Russell into a lizard when he caught her. Emerson laughed so hard he choked on his wine. Russell, who had not said anything all dinner, muttered, "Wasn't funny. . . . It took weeks before I could get the taste of flies out of my mouth."

It was late when people started to leave the table to get some rest before the big day tomorrow. Annabelle thanked everyone again, smiled at Nick, and then went to her room.

Rosie was still sound asleep on the floor. Annabelle double-checked her pack again and then paced the room, nervously thinking about tomorrow. Just as she lay down and pulled the quilt up to her chin, she heard a knock on her door. Rosie sighed and opened her eyes sleepily.

Annabelle climbed out of bed and cracked the door open.

"I just wanted to see you one more time before the big day tomorrow," Nick said, taking Annabelle's hand in his. "I am so glad our paths have crossed again. I knew you were special." He brought her hand up to his lips and softly kissed it.

Annabelle held her breath. She could feel her cheeks burning as she blushed. "I am, too, Nick. Thank you for coming with me."

"Of course, Princess. Good night," Nick said, bowing as he shut her bedroom door.

Annabelle sighed; she could feel the butterflies in her stomach. She climbed back into bed and closed her eyes. "This is going to work," she told herself. She couldn't imagine leaving this world behind.

Chapter 12

Ann awoke before the sun came up. She sat up in bed and looked around. She almost felt disoriented, trying to remember where she was. She was feeling more and more like this was the dream, and the world with her father was reality. Worry crept into her heart. What if it happens that she can't travel back to this world? How would her mother handle not only losing her husband but her daughter as well? She shook the thoughts out of her head. She couldn't think like that. There was still hope!

She climbed out of bed and met her mom downstairs in the kitchen. "Good morning, sweetie," Ann's mom said, giving her a hug. "You look well rested today."

Ann smiled. "I am. But I'm not sure I'm ready to go back to school." She opened the fridge, pulled out a smoothie, and sat down at the table. Her mom brought her some toast and scrambled eggs.

"Reality can be harsh sometimes!" her mom said, kissing her on the top of her head. "I have to get going, but I hope you have a good day. Don't be late!"

"Thank you, Mom," Ann said, taking a bite of the

toast. She quickly finished breakfast, got dressed, and hurried out the door, grabbing her backpack on the way. Her rusty old pickup truck was waiting in the driveway.

By the time she got to school the first bell was ringing. She met her friends in the hallway, making some small talk about the weekend and whether they were nervous about finals. She then headed to her first class of the day, calculus with Mr. Pothoven.

"Good morning, Ann," Mr. Pothoven said as she walked into his classroom. "You look well rested today."

"I am, thank you," Ann said, smiling. He was a good teacher. She always appreciated the effort he made to help each student in understanding his lessons.

The final bell rang, and Mr. Pothoven handed out the tests. "Good luck, everyone. I hope that you all studied your notes this weekend."

The rest of Ann's classes went by slowly. She was anxious to get home and see her mom. It seemed like so much of her life that she worried about felt so insignificant now. When school let out Ann headed straight to her car. Usually her friends would get together at one of the lunch tables to talk. But today, she didn't want to talk to them about school gossip or picking a date for the dance. She just wanted to figure out a way to not lose one of her worlds, one of her parents, forever.

When Ann got home, she sat with her mom in the living room on their cozy brown sectional sofa for a while. They talked about school and how finals went. "I already did chores for Lucy today; I figured you would have a lot of studying to do tonight," her mom said, getting off the couch and heading to the kitchen.

"Mom," Ann said, biting her cheek nervously.

"Yes, sweetie?" she asked, leaning back into the living room.

"Can I look through the wedding pictures of you and dad?"

There was a pause, and then her mom walked back into the room. "Yes, of course, Ann," she said, tucking her brown hair behind her ear. "The album is in my room, in the drawer of the bedside table."

"Thank you," Ann said, scooting off the couch. She stopped and petted Cleo, who was sleeping soundly on the recliner. Cleo opened her eyes to scowl at Ann for waking her up, and then went back to sleep.

Ann took the album to her room. She crossed her legs on her bed and put the album in her lap. She studied the book. It was trimmed with ivory lace. The front picture was black and white, a picture of her mom leaning against her dad; they both were smiling from ear to ear. She traced her fingers over the gold lettering: "James and Lori Lexington," then slowly flipped through the pages. She studied the faces of her parents, how happy they looked. She stopped on one of the pictures, a photo of her dad with Aunt Ester. Aunt Ester looked much younger, and much happier. Her hair was a rich, chestnut brown in the picture, just like her dad's. She had a colorful bouquet of flowers and she was in a bright turquoise bridesmaid's dress.

"That is your dad's sister, Ester," Ann's mom said.

Ann jumped in surprise; she hadn't heard her mom come in. She was standing beside the bed, a bowl of broccoli-cheese soup in her hands.

"I don't know if you remember her. She disappeared before your father did," her mom continued, scooting herself on the bed beside Ann and putting the bowl of soup on Ann's bedside table. "You look a lot like her, and your father, too." Ann's mom lifted her hand and carefully used one of her thin, elegant fingers to trace around Ann's father's face in the photo. "I always wondered if they found each other somewhere." She was silent for a moment, staring sadly at the picture. She rested her head on Ann's shoulder and then flipped to the next page. They looked through the rest of the album together in silence.

When they got to the end, Ann slowly shut the book and handed it to her mom, who hugged it to her chest. "I know he loved you, Mom," Ann said, looking into her mom's face. Her eyes looked distant, like she was miles away.

Ann's voice brought her mom back to reality. "I know, sweetie," she said, smiling sadly. "I am going to clean up the kitchen, enjoy the sunset, and get some sleep. I love you," she said, kissing Ann on the forehead.

"I love you too, Mom," Ann said, picking up the bowl of soup. "Thank you for making me dinner."

"Of course, sweetie," her mom said, shutting the door to Ann's room as she left.

Ann ate dinner in her room and then headed downstairs to put the empty bowl in the kitchen sink. She paused to look out the living room window at her mom. She was sitting in her rocking chair on the front porch with a cup of tea, looking down the lane. Ann put the bowl and spoon in the sink and went back up to her room, a knot in her stomach. She avoided looking out the window as she climbed the stairs to her room and wished with all her heart that she could bring her father back to her mom.

Ann opened her backpack and pulled out a textbook. She spread out her notes on her bed and spent a few hours studying. Cleo jumped on her bed and climbed over her backpack and on top of her textbook, letting Ann know that it was bedtime. "Okay, okay," Ann said, shutting the book and stretching her arms. She changed into pajamas and brushed her teeth. Ann repacked her backpack and adjusted her blankets on her bed. "Good night, Cleo," Ann said, kissing her on the head and curling up in bed.

Chapter 13

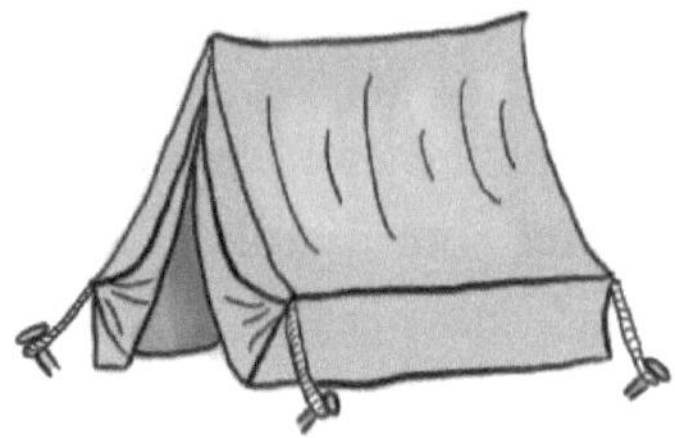

Annabelle woke up to muffled voices in the hallway outside her room. She could hear several people talking. She lay in bed a minute, trying to make out what they were saying. When she decided she couldn't hear anything discernible, she climbed out of bed. She picked out one of her cotton dresses—a green one for luck—and her Aunt Ester's mink shawl. Aunt Ester had lent it to her for warmth on the trip. She woke Rosie up and picked up her pack. Annabelle opened the door to the hallway and stepped out.

There were several people moving about in the hallway, all with arms full of blankets and food and other various packages. When they caught sight of Annabelle, they all paused to bow and wish her good morning, and then continued out the front door.

Annabelle followed them, with Rosie on her heels. They were loading up a small wagon. There were two palomino horses hooked up to the wagon. She went up and rubbed the muzzle of one of the horses.

"Good morning, Annabelle!" Whitney called from

behind her.

"Whitney!" Annabelle exclaimed, turning around to see her friend. "I was hoping I would get to see you before I left today."

"I was hoping to see you, too! Emerson invited me to dinner, but I was busy helping pack and prepare for today. I just met with your father; he should be here before you leave. He was just checking on his horses in the barn." Whitney put the bucket she was carrying in the wagon with a thud, and then brushed off her hands on her dress. Her blonde hair was braided loosely behind her back. "This is the wagon that your group will be taking. There will also be a few other horses. You wouldn't all want to cram into this little wagon, that would be one uncomfortable ride. It isn't a carriage by any means, but it is very reliable."

"Thank you, Whitney. Emerson has done so much for me already."

"Your father has fought for his town countless times. Emerson would go to the end of the earth for King James," Whitney said. "I know Nick is pretty excited to go with you, too." She looked at Annabelle as she said this, an ornery smirk on her face.

Annabelle blushed and hid her face. "I am happy he is coming, too."

Annabelle looked up to see Russell, Gary, and Merry Anne gathered together behind the wagon. They were talking quietly among themselves. She was about to walk over to join them when she caught sight of her father walking from the barn with Emerson, and Nick behind them with two horses in tow. She smiled, relieved to be able to see her dad one more time before her journey.

Nick handed Merry Anne the reins to one of the horses he was leading, and the other to Gary. Annabelle walked over to Merry Anne's white horse with black speckles. The horse was missing an ear.

Merry Anne grinned as Annabelle studied her horse. "This is Lace," Merry Anne said. "She has been my traveling partner for as long as I've been traveling. She's quite the escape artist. Lost her ear trying to roll under a fence." Merry Anne patted the horse on her side.

They all gathered around the wagon. Emerson made a speech that Annabelle was too nervous to comprehend. Her father thanked everyone, shaking their hands one by one. When he came to face Annabelle, she could see the look of worry in his eyes. He petted Rosie's head roughly and said, "Keep an eye on Annabelle for me, you little mutt. We looked around the market for you for quite some time yesterday." He dropped his hand from Rosie's head to Annabelle's shoulder. "Please be safe, my dear," her father said, hugging her closely.

"I will be," Annabelle squeaked out, trying to hold back her tears. She put Rosie down and hugged him once more, then followed Russell and Nick to the wagon. Annabelle picked up Rosie again, whose face was covered in dust. Nick climbed in the wagon and took the reins. Russell turned to Annabelle. He was slightly shorter than her, and very stocky. Being a man of very few words, he smiled, helped Annabelle into the wagon, and climbed in the back with the supplies.

Annabelle held Rosie on her lap and looked back to wave goodbye to her father and Emerson. She watched until they faded into the distance. Soon she couldn't even see Emerson's mansion.

They rode in silence awhile, just listening to the sound of the horse's hooves on the dirt road and watching the trees pass by. Rosie was asleep on Annabelle's lap. Annabelle clung to her like a life preserver, the only reminder of home that she had.

They had passed through several small towns as the sun began to set. The rolling hills had turned to flat, open plains. Annabelle couldn't believe how far in the distance she could see. The wagon came to a stop.

"We should be to the Enchanted Forest tomorrow," Merry Anne said, stopping her horse beside the wagon. "Let's camp here tonight. If we pushed it, we could probably get to the edge of the forest tonight, but it's best not to sleep too close to it."

Russell tossed blankets and stakes out of the back of the wagon to the ground with a thud. Nick hopped out of the wagon and held his hand to help Annabelle as she climbed out behind him. The dry golden-yellow grass crunched noisily under their feet as everyone worked in silence, setting up small makeshift tents for the night. Rosie ran anxiously around camp, sniffing the ground. Gary and Merry Anne unsaddled the horses and tied them to a couple of nearby trees next to a creek so they could get a nice cool drink of water. Russell started a fire while Nick and Annabelle pulled fruit and a couple jars of canned meat out of one of the packs from the back of the wagon.

After the camp was put together, everyone sat around the fire. Merry Anne shared stories about the witch they were seeking while the food was eaten. "We won't find her unless she lets us find her. I can get us close, but she has an ability to cloak herself from people passing by. She is very secretive and keeps herself fairly isolated. She is the most powerful witch left in this world."

When the darkness of night engulfed the group, and thousands of stars were peeking through the clouds, just the light of the campfire illuminated the silhouettes of Annabelle's traveling group. Silence fell over them as they listened to the distant calls of the wild animals surrounding them.

Annabelle heard the crunching of grass as a low crouched figure in the dark came running toward the campfire. She gasped in surprise. Russell stood up, his hand on his sword, ready to scare off whatever it was. When it got close enough to the light, Merry Anne let out a laugh. Rosie was back, with a dead rat for dinner. Slowly, everyone headed to their little tents for the night. Annabelle smiled warmly at Nick as she crawled into her tent. Russell sat by the fire, his back resting against a tree. Annabelle closed her eyes and listened to the chorus of the wind through the grass, the call of the wild animals, and the patter of the water running down the creek and was slowly lulled to sleep.

Chapter 14

"Ann, you're going to be late to school," Ann's mom called from the stairs. "Breakfast is ready downstairs. I have to get going."

Ann rolled from her side to her back. She had hit snooze on her alarm clock several times, not ready to face the morning. Another day of finals in this world. She climbed out of bed and pulled a sweatshirt out from under Cleo, who laid her ears back and frowned in protest.

On the way to school Ann found herself thinking about her father in the other world. She wondered if her dad ever missed driving this old pickup truck, which once was his. Ann remembered watching him work on it, parked in the front yard with the hood up while she would ride her bike around the driveway. Her mom would come wrap her arms around his waist and rest her head between his shoulder blades, listening to his heartbeat.

She shook those thoughts away as she pulled into the school parking lot and saw her friends, Grace and Noah, who were walking into the school. They paused to wait for Ann. She put the truck into park and pulled her bag out of the passenger seat. Ann greeted her friends with a warm smile. "Thank you for waiting for me, guys," she said, putting one of her arms around each of their shoulders. "One day of finals down, one more to go!"

Noah smiled. "It's going to be a good day!" he said, breaking off from the group as they got into the school to head to his first class. "I'll see you guys at lunch."

Grace and Ann headed to class together, talking about college plans and dorm-room shopping. It was hard for Ann to imagine her future here. If she lost the ability to travel and stayed in this world, could she just live the rest of her life as if traveling to another world had never happened? This world would never understand the other life she was living. And her father would never see her graduate from high school or help her move into college.

By the time the day was over, Ann's head was spinning. She was worn out from tests and was getting nervous about going back to the other world. Ann struggled to focus on taking her finals. Hopefully soon she would have some answers to her growing number of questions. After school she made a point to sit at the lunchroom table to chat with her friend Megan, and soon was joined by Grace and Noah. After catching up on some of the gossip, she picked up her backpack and told her friends goodbye and that she would see them next week. Then she headed home to spend some time with her mom.

Ann pulled up to her house. She sat in the truck and listened to the end of her favorite song. As she turned the engine off, she pulled her backpack out of the passenger seat and slung it over her shoulder. She stepped onto the porch and paused, hearing Lucy's whinny coming from the backyard.

She dumped her backpack into the old rocking chair and headed to the backyard. When she got there, she leaned against the back of the house beside her mom's white trellis. It was covered in magenta petunias that twisted their way to the very top. She watched her mom ride Lucy around the yard. Ann smiled, happy to see her mom enjoying herself. She had seemed sad lately.

Ann's mom looked up and waved at Ann, just now realizing that her daughter was watching her. She trotted Lucy up to the house and climbed down from the saddle. "How was your day?" she asked, hugging Ann tightly.

"Good! I survived finals, anyway!" Ann said, smiling.

They walked Lucy back to the barn together, talking about their days and how much Lucy had learned this past year. She was one of their best horses.

When Ann got into the house, she kicked her shoes off and went into the kitchen to start dinner. She had the water boiling and sauce heating up for spaghetti by the time her mom got inside.

"Good choice, sweetie," her mom said, patting her on the back and sitting at the kitchen table.

They talked about her mom's work and Ann's thoughts about college as Ann stirred in the spaghetti noodles and popped the garlic bread into the oven. It wasn't long until the mouthwatering smell of the garlic bread was rolling out of the oven, and when the timer went off, Ann's stomach was growling.

Her mom had set the table, and when Ann brought the bread and spaghetti over, they sat down and ate, enjoying the meal together.

After dinner Ann's mom made herself a cup of mint tea and walked over to the front door. "Would you like to join me on the porch?" she called to Ann.

Ann hesitated for a minute. In her heart she was dying to tell her mom everything: all about her dad and the other world. But what if her mom thought she was crazy? Ann even felt she was going crazy sometimes. If it weren't for the twine bracelet Nick gave her, tightly tied to her wrist, she wouldn't believe it herself. She twirled the bracelet around her arm a few times and then nodded her head. "Yes, Mom, I will meet you out there once I get the dishes done."

They sat and watched the sunset. The brilliant pinks and oranges slowly turned to deep blues and purples as the sun disappeared and the stars started to come out.

"I had better get my homework done. Once I finish this college credit, I am in the clear! I love you," Ann said, kissing her mom on the forehead and heading into the house.

"I love you, too, Ann," her mom called as Ann shut the screen door behind her.

Ann sat on her bed in her room, all her homework was spread across her bed, biting on one of her fingernails. She was so mad at herself for not being able to share this with her mom. One of the biggest events in her life and she felt like she had no one in this world to share it with.

After a few hours Ann packed her homework up and curled up in her bed. Then she wrapped her arm around Cleo, who had snuck under the sheets while Ann was changing into her pajamas. It didn't take long until she was fast asleep.

Chapter 15

Annabelle woke up to a loud clatter. She quickly climbed out of her small tent to see what the noise was. The sun was barely rising, and it was still dark around their campsite. She could see Russell's stalky silhouette by the wagon as he was noisily tossing various items into the back of it. Rosie whined in protest as she climbed out of the tent as well, stretched, and ran off toward where the horses were tied.

"Good morning, Princess," Merry Anne said, walking toward Annabelle with her hands full of folded linens from her tent. "I hope you slept well."

"I did; thank you, Merry Anne," Annabelle said, smiling warmly.

Annabelle took down her tent with Merry Anne's help. They proceeded in dismantling the remaining tents as Russell cooked breakfast over the dwindling fire.

Everyone gathered around the fire and quickly ate breakfast. Annabelle was anxious to get going. She was ready to find this witch and see the Enchanted Forest.

Gary stood up and walked over to where the horses were tied. He hitched them up to the wagon and handed Lace's reins to Merry Anne. As Russell and Nick climbed into the wagon, Annabelle paced around the campsite, calling for Rosie. She put her hands on her hips, looking out past the creek. She didn't know where that dog ran off to. Annabelle whistled, trying to call Rosie back to her. She turned back to the wagon and walked slowly to the group. She didn't know what to do; if they waited any longer it would take time away from the trip, and if she left, what would happen to Rosie?

Annabelle got to the wagon and looked at Nick. "I— I'm not sure where Rosie is," she said, tears starting to well up in her eyes.

"We will find her, Annabelle," Nick said, scanning the area.

Annabelle gave one more whistle, her stomach in knots. She stood for what seemed like hours listening for Rosie. And then there she was, running up the side of the creek, barking. Annabelle let out a sigh of relief as she picked up her dog. "You should have stayed in the carriage back in Emerson's Town," Annabelle said, scolding Rosie. "I just knew you were going to be trouble." Rosie put her ears back, as if she knew she was in trouble, and laid her head on Annabelle's shoulder.

They climbed into the wagon and continued their journey to the Enchanted Forest. At first, they rode in silence, just listening to the sound of the horses' hooves on the dirt road. Annabelle looked to the back of the wagon and caught Russell staring at her. He looked down at his hands at first, in embarrassment. But then he quickly looked back up, curiosity getting the best of him. "Tell us Annabelle. . . . What is your other world like?"

"Russell," Gary said sternly, giving him a scolding look. "You know we don't need to know that."

Russell twisted his mouth in annoyance. "I know . . ."

"I would love to share," Annabelle said, smiling in amusement.

The time went by quickly as Annabelle shared stories about her mother, school, and technology. The group was amazed by the internet. Russell kept repeating, "It's like an invisible farmer's market."

"We are nearing the forest," Merry Anne said, pulling a compass out from under her coat. It was on a long chain around her neck. She glanced at it and then tucked it away again.

Annabelle heard a raspy whisper behind her, "*I am waiting for you, Annabelle.*" It was a familiar woman's voice. She turned to look, but all she saw was Russell, looking intently at her, waiting to hear more of her other world stories.

"Did you hear that?" Annabelle asked him.

Russell raised his eyebrows in confusion. "What?" he asked.

She looked at Nick, who shrugged his shoulders. "I didn't hear anything either."

Annabelle shook her head; maybe she just imagined it.

"*Annabelle!*" the voice hissed, echoing in her ears, making the hair on the back of her neck stand up and sending goosebumps down her arms. She bit the inside of her cheek. This time she didn't say anything to anyone. Best not to make the group worry.

The wagon stopped abruptly. Annabelle looked up to

see they had just crept into the dark, looming forest. The path darkened quickly as the sun was swallowed up by the tall trees. Rosie shivered on Annabelle's lap, letting out a low whimper as she laid her ears flat. The horses acted nervous; their eyes open wide. They were quick to spook over just the wind blowing through the leaves of the nearby trees.

Merry Anne jumped off Lace and pulled some green herbs out of her saddle bag. She fed some to each of the horses. "It's just a little concoction I made; it will calm their nerves. They won't be as stealthy, but at least we won't have to worry about them running away in a panic. Who knows where they would end up? Horses don't like the feel of these woods." She patted her Lace on the shoulder and then climbed back on. "We are ready to go."

Nick flicked the reins and the wagon started moving again, at a slower pace. The path was rough and narrow. Merry Anne took the lead, while Gary rode behind the wagon. Annabelle could hear Gary and Russell's voices, but the rattle of the wagon wheels over the bumpy path drowned out what they were saying.

The forest was dark and eerie. Annabelle could hear various animals calling out to each other. Her eyes still had not adjusted to the dark haze that swallowed them. There was no sneaking through the forest; the wagon's wheels noisily struggled over hundreds of tree roots that had grown into the path. Every living creature in the forest was aware of their presence now.

Annabelle saw a large brown snake coiled around one of the low-hanging branches of a tree leaning over the path. She ducked her head as the wagon crossed under it. Every vine that grazed her arms or tangled in her hair after that, she thought for sure it was a snake. Bugs swarmed around them, buzzing in their ears and biting at their exposed skin. She wrapped her aunt's mink shawl tightly over her shoulders, covering up as much of her skin as possible from the biting pests. Annabelle closed her eyes, trying to block out the snakes and the bugs, two things she was comfortable living without when she was tucked away in the castle.

Suddenly, the wagon plummeted to the ground with a crash. Annabelle bit her tongue as she slammed against the wagon seat when it hit the ground. Blankets, food, and supplies flew up into the air and littered the forest floor around the group. Annabelle looked from Russell to Nick in surprise, dazed and unsure of what happened. Nick's eyes met hers as he jumped up from the wagon seat and pulled his bow and arrows from under the seat.

"Wood elves!" Nick shouted.

Annabelle stood up, pushing Rosie off her lap. She could hear what sounded like children squealing with laughter as she watched the wagon wheels disappear through the trees, carried off by little creatures, barely taller than the wheels they were hauling away. Their skin looked like tree bark; their clothing looked as if it was made from green tree moss.

"Those sly creatures," Russell said, rubbing his back sorely as he slowly stood up from the wagon.

"What just happened?!" Annabelle demanded, looking down at Russell as he bent over to examine a broken jar of preserves that had shattered in the back of the wagon.

"Wood elves," Russell said, tossing the broken jar to the ground. "And thanks to them we will have more days in this forest than any of us wanted."

"No, it means she is close," Merry Anne said, climbing off her saddle to help sift through the rubble. "We will salvage what we can and then keep moving."

"What is a wood elf?" Annabelle asked, still trying to process what just happened.

"They're the forest pranksters," Gary replied, putting his sword back in its scabbard and putting some salvaged food into one of his saddlebags. "Rare. I haven't seen any in years. They are drawn to magic, typically working for the witch we are looking for. They have the ability to use some magic, but it is drawn from her. I'm sure magic played a role in the little prank they just pulled."

The group searched through the supplies that were scattered about the forest around them. "We will have to travel a lot lighter now," Merry Anne said, glancing carefully around the forest. "We don't want to overload the horses."

Russell unhitched the horses and sighed. "I hate riding horses," he muttered, handing one set of reins to Nick and then slowly pulling himself onto the back of the other horse.

"It looks like we will be sharing this one," Nick said, gracefully climbing onto the back of the horse. He held out his hand and pulled Annabelle up behind him.

They rode in silence. No more stories were shared, and Annabelle felt as though the dark of the forest added weight to the air around them. Russell made a point to stay toward the back of the group, while Gary stayed close to Annabelle, their eyes darting around the trees, trying to stay alert for whatever else was coming their way. Rosie followed on the ground; her ears nervously laid back flat as she worked to stay close to the horse Annabelle was riding.

The group never stopped for lunch. Their anxiousness to get out of the forest kept them pushing forward. But soon it grew dark and they had to face the fact that they were going to be spending the night in the forest.

Merry Anne stopped her horse and turned around to face the group. She looked from Nick to Russell. "We will have to find a place to camp. It needs to be close to the path but out of sight. Based on some of the tracks I've seen, we aren't the only ones traveling on it."

Russell nodded, steering his horse off the path. "It looks like there's a little clearing over here."

The group followed Russell's lead. Quietly, they set up the tents. Gary handed out some of the bread and jerky that he had in his saddlebag to each person. "No fire tonight, we don't want to draw any more attention to ourselves."

Annabelle looked around the trees looming over them. The full moon's light peeked through each of the knotted, twisted trees, giving them an eerie silhouette.

After a while of eating in silence, Nick stood up and cleared his throat. "Best we get some sleep. Russell, would you mind keeping first watch?"

"My pleasure," Russell said, standing up. He clapped his hand on Nick's shoulder as he passed him to sit against a nearby tree. "I don't imagine anyone will get much sleep tonight anyway."

Annabelle climbed into her tent, pulling Rosie tightly to her chest. There were no noises in the night. No animals calling to each other, no bugs singing. Just a deafening silence. She lay in her tent, staring into the darkness.

"*Annabelle*," the raspy, eerie voice called, "*this journey is your own.*"

Annabelle sat up, digging her fingers into Rosie's fur. Rosie's ears trembled nervously.

"*Leave.*"

Annabelle covered her ears, trying to block out the voice.

"*If you want the answers you seek, you cannot be weak.*" The raspy voice flooded into her mind, loud and clear.

Annabelle bit the inside of her cheek nervously, and she slowly climbed out of her tent, her knees weak. Her hands shook as she pulled her aunt's shawl over her shoulders. She picked up her little canvas bag she had packed for the journey and glanced over to the tree that Russell had picked to lean against while he kept watch. He wasn't there! Annabelle choked on the cold air she had just breathed in. She forced herself to walk over to the tree. A pile of clothes sat at the base of it, Russell's clothes. She sifted through them to find the little knife he had always carried at his waist. Her hands touched something cold and slimy. She picked it up and held it up to her face. It was a small toad. The scowl on its little face instantly confirmed what she already knew—it was Russell. She put his knife in her pack and Russell in the pocket of her shawl. "Sorry, Russell," she whispered, as she started to walk into the darkness, away from her traveling group, back to the path. She refused to look back. She didn't want to see the tents where the people that cared about her slept. Nick, Merry Anne, and Gary will be baffled when they wake up to find her gone. What will they think? After everything they were willing to do for her. . . . After all the miles they had traveled together. . . .

The silvery moon lit the path. "I don't even know where to go," she said quietly to herself, finally taking a second to look back. The trees and darkness swallowed any chance she had of seeing the tents where her friends lay sleeping. "At least they won't be discovered there," she said, continuing on the path.

The sound of footsteps running up behind her made Annabelle spin around, her heart in her throat. She thought for sure someone from the group had seen her leaving.

Rosie leaped into Annabelle's arms, licking her face. Annabelle smiled. "Hopefully you don't count when I was told to come alone," she said to Rosie, petting the top of her head.

Annabelle and Rosie continued on until the sun was breaking through the trees and touching the dirt path. She felt a little better to be walking in the dim light of the morning sun. Although it wasn't much brighter than the moon, she could see farther down the path than she could before.

Soon, Annabelle came to a fork in the road. She paused, unsure of which way to go. "*Trust your feet*," the voice echoed into her head.

"Well what does that even mean?" Annabelle asked, scrunching up her face in annoyance.

Rosie tilted her head up at Annabelle, a confused look on her face.

Annabelle closed her eyes and walked on. The path led her to a meadow. She followed another winding path. She guessed it was about noon when she came to a creek brimming with water. She followed the creek downhill to a small cottage. Annabelle could see smoke rolling from the chimney. She let out a sigh. Her adrenaline was pumping now.

Even though she had not slept, she was wide awake. She pulled Russell out of her pocket and looked at his angry little face. "I promise, by the end of this, you will be back to normal again. Although, you do make a pretty cute toad." She tucked him back into her pocket and jogged the rest of the way to the cottage. Vines engulfed it, wrapping around the walls and climbing hungrily on the roof. Annabelle was afraid to take her eyes off the house. It was almost as if the vines would swallow it right before her very eyes.

The door opened as she approached. A young woman stood in the doorway, a welcoming smile on her face. "Good afternoon, traveler!" she called.

Annabelle's heart dropped to her stomach. This was not the raspy-voiced woman that had been calling to her. Her feet had led her astray. She left her group behind, only to get lost.

"You look tired. Don't just stand in the front yard with the trees, come and have a cup of tea," the young woman said, leaving the door open and walking farther into the cottage.

Part of Annabelle wanted to just leave, go back to the woods and try again. But her feet ached, and her energy was gone. All she wanted to do now was sleep. Her mind drifted. She wondered if her mother was worried about her. Did she go to her daughter's bedroom to find it empty? Would her mom think she ran away? Annabelle shook the thoughts out of her head and walked into the cottage.

The inside of the cottage was surprisingly bright and clean. She walked down the hallway and into a small kitchen. The young woman had her back to Annabelle. "Have a seat, please. This should be ready soon."

Annabelle sat heavily onto one of the little wooden chairs that was sitting in the corner of the kitchen. She watched the young woman work; she had a very small build. Her curly jet-black hair was blowing with the breeze coming from the window by the counter where she worked.

"Where do you come from?" the woman asked, turning around to rest her eyes on Annabelle.

Annabelle paused for a minute, unsure of what to tell her. "It is a small town far away from here."

The young woman smiled. Her gray-green eyes were familiar to Annabelle. "I don't see many people coming and going around here. The forest is not a place people choose to come to willingly." She poured two cups of tea and handed one to Annabelle.

"And yet you live here?" Annabelle asked, taking the cup of tea from the young woman.

"Yes," the woman said, sweeping her deep-purple dress to the side as she sat in the chair beside Annabelle. "This has always been my home. My parents built it, raised my brother and me here, and eventually died here." She paused and took a sip of her tea. "I couldn't imagine living anywhere else. The forest is dangerous, but it is also full of so much wonder."

Annabelle glanced out the window at the sun slowly fading behind the clouds. Half the day had gone so quickly, and she had not ended up where she needed to be. She was tired now, her eyes heavy. She stifled a yawn and smiled at the woman as she drank another sip of tea. "Thank you for your hospitality. I really should be on my way . . ." But to where? Her feet did not lead her where she needed to go.

"Why don't you rest for a while? You look like you haven't slept in days. I have a room ready for you."

Annabelle smiled again, putting down her cup. "Sleep sounds amazing. Thank you."

The young woman led Annabelle through the cottage to a dimly lit bedroom and shut the door behind her as she left. Annabelle knew better than to stay at a stranger's house, but she was so tired. As she lay down in bed and quickly fell asleep, one last thought came through her head: "If she didn't have a lot of people passing by here, why did she have a bed made up for me?"

Chapter 16

"ANN JEANNE LEXINGTON!!" Ann shot out of her bed, her feet barely touching the ground at the sound of her mother's shrieking voice.

"Mom?" Ann replied, knowing her mother was going to be upset with her. She missed half a day in this world. Her mom was probably worried sick.

"Where have you been? I called all your friends' houses, I looked everywhere—I even called the police! If you were at that party the police broke up last night, you are so incredibly grounded! This close to graduation and you want to ruin everything you have worked so hard for?!" Ann's mother scolded, walking into Ann's room. "And now I hear you moving about in your room when it's almost evening!"

"Mom, I'm so sorry. I—"

"Save it. I want you to seriously think about your choices." Her mom paused for a moment, looking at her daughter, her hands tightly gripping both of Ann's shoulders. Her anger broke into tears. "I am so glad you are safe," she said, hugging Ann closely, tears welling up in her eyes. "I don't know what I would do if I lost you too."

"I am safe. I'm okay. I'm sorry, Mom." Ann hugged her mom back, feeling terrible. How would her mom ever believe the truth?

"You need a shower. You smell like you've been rolling in the dirt. I will fix us something to eat. Come down after your shower."

Ann smiled. If she could only tell her where she has been! "Okay, Mom," she said, heading to the bathroom.

After her shower, Ann held her clean clothes up to her nose and breathed in the fresh smell of laundry detergent. It's funny how quickly she missed the comforts of home. She ran down the stairs, her feet barely touching the steps. She had to tell her mom today! She couldn't talk herself out of it again. Ann stopped right before she got into the kitchen. She could hear voices; her mom was talking to someone else.

She went in to see her mom sitting at their kitchen table with Officer Andrews. Ann bit her cheek in annoyance. Wonderful. He had been trying to date her mother the minute her mom called the police to say Dad was missing.

"Ann Lexington!" Officer Andrews announced, standing up from the table so quickly that his large belly made a full glass of water sitting on the table spill. "Oh Lori, I am so sorry," he said, trying to mop up the mess with a napkin.

"Tyler. What brings you to our house?" Ann asked, raising her eyebrows at him.

"*Officer Andrews* was just checking in to see whether

you made it home safely," her mom said, giving Ann the you-had-better-quit-it, you're-already-in-trouble look.

"How kind of you," Ann said, smiling a fake smile at him.

"Just doing my job," Officer Andrews said, putting his hat back on and scooting the chair he was sitting in back under the table. "I hate to see your mother worry."

"Of course you do," Ann said, quickly adding, "I'm sure all the officers have that concern for the citizens of their community."

Ann's mom gave her another angry look and handed Tyler a plate full of cookies. "Please, share these with the other officers that took time out of their schedule to look for my up-to-no-good daughter."

"I sure will, Lori," Tyler said, letting his hand linger too long on Ann's mom's as he took the plate from her. Ann rolled her eyes. "It's always a pleasure to see you."

Ann and her mom walked Officer Andrews to the door and he slowly pulled out of their driveway, waving as he left.

"So . . . ," Ann said, letting the silence drag on for a minute. "You really want to be his third wife?"

"You really are looking for trouble today, aren't you?" her mom asked, scowling at Ann. "He is just doing his job."

"Yeah, I bet," Ann replied.

They sat at the table and ate supper quietly. Ann had wanted so much to tell her mom about what had been going on. But Officer Andrews ruined her moment. What if her mother would rather be with Tyler than her father? No way. No one is better for her than Ann's dad. Ann shook her head, stabbing a few peas with her fork in frustration.

"I am going to bed," her mom said, putting her fork down noisily. "I expect an explanation of what happened in the morning. I am just too tired to keep being angry. Please clean up dinner. And oh, I would like you to be in your bed when I come to your room in the morning, if that is not too much to ask."

"Yes, Mom, I will," Ann said, "Thank you. I love you."

Her mom walked out of the room, not saying another word to Ann.

Ann sat quietly at the table. She knew her mom was really hurting.

"I love you, too," she heard her mom call from the bedroom.

Ann smiled—at least her mom wasn't that mad. She cleaned up the kitchen and decided to watch some television. After flipping through the channels several times, Ann sighed and put the remote down. It was hard to even enjoy watching a show when her own life was so full of mystery. Ann walked over to the mahogany colored bookshelf tucked in the corner of the living room. She smiled as she found her mother's senior yearbook. Ann pulled it out and flipped through it until she came across her mother and father's class picture. She scowled at Officer Andrews's picture. "I wonder if he was trying to date you even when Dad was around," Ann said out loud.

"He wasn't," Ann's mom said, startling Ann so much that she almost dropped the book. "He dated your Aunt Ester."

Ann laughed, "Seriously?"

Ann's mom nodded. "She was older than your dad, but any chance Officer Andrews could, he would try to stop by their house to see if she was home from college. Sorry to startle you; I just needed a glass of water," Ann's mom kissed Ann on the forehead. "Good night."

Ann put the yearbook back on the shelf. She changed the channel on the television a few more times, still unable to focus on anything. She turned it off and stretched. Ann restlessly walked around the house. She felt anxious, unsure of what to do with herself. When she finally sat down, she found herself outside on the front porch, sitting in her mom's rocking chair.

The air was crisp and cool outside. In the distance a deer and her twin fawns were just coming out to eat. The fawns were so small, white spots still speckled their backs. The deer cautiously walked out of the timber, looking around for any danger. Ann could hear Lucy whinnying excitedly at them.

Ann walked to the barn to visit Lucy. She fed her an extra scoop of grain and rubbed her nose lovingly while Lucy nuzzled her head against Ann. Ann hugged Lucy around the neck and breathed in the smell of the barn; the mix of hay and horse was one of her favorite combinations. Ann stayed in the barn for a while, brushing Lucy's coat and mane. When Lucy finished eating, Ann went back to the pasture to see the deer, and then headed to the house.

Ann stood on the porch and watched as the deer finished eating. She opened the screen door and walked back into the house. Ann turned the lights off before she headed to her room, pausing at the stairs to look at all the family pictures that filled the stairway. She touched one picture of her mom and dad, outside their house. The roof was covered with snow and Christmas lights. This picture was all that remained of the last year they spent together, and the last year they had covered this old farmhouse with lights. She yawned and rubbed her eyes, then headed the rest of the way upstairs.

Her cat, Cleo, was already on Ann's pillow when she got to her room, sound asleep. Ann scooted under her blankets and laid her head on the pillow beside Cleo, who opened one eye to glare at Ann for disturbing her. Quickly, Ann drifted off to sleep.

Chapter 17

Annabelle woke up to the sound of familiar childish laughter. She had heard it in the forest, when the wood elves were running off with their wagon wheels. She stood up quickly, grabbing her bag she had placed at the end of her bed and bolting out of the room. She could hear her heartbeat in her ears. If the wood elves were here, what if they hurt that young woman who gave her a place to rest? Not only did she get herself lost but now she put someone else in danger, too.

When she got to the kitchen, she looked around. The room was dark. Annabelle stumbled into the next small room, and then the next. Her eyes struggled to adjust to the darkness. When she first arrived, it had seemed so bright and cheery. "Hello?" Annabelle called, starting to wonder where the woman had gone.

"Annabelle," the woman called, "I'm outside in the garden."

Annabelle found her way outside to find the young woman, who was kneeling down in the dirt, two baskets full of beautiful fruits and vegetables beside her. Rosie was running around the garden, chasing bugs.

"Are you okay?" Annabelle asked, looking around the trees nervously.

"Of course," the woman said, standing up and brushing the dirt off her hands. "And good morning to you. You must have been tired, you slept all through the evening and the night! Let's go inside. Could you please grab one of the baskets?"

Annabelle picked up one of the baskets and followed the woman into her house, but stopped the minute she stepped through the doorway. She had walked into a huge room, the walls were floor-to-ceiling shelves filled with books and glass jars, and there was a large cast-iron caldron in the center of the room. A brass chandelier hung from the ceiling. Annabelle dropped the basket she was holding in surprise. "What on earth?—"

The woman turned to face Annabelle; she had a smile on her face. Her grey-green eyes gleamed brightly. "I had to wait for my wood elves' report. I didn't want them interrupting us, but I also needed to know if your friends were close. It sounds like they will need you soon."

"My friends need me?" Annabelle asked, trying to process this. "How do you know about them?"

"Oh, Annabelle. You are smart. Do not doubt your intuition."

Annabelle walked past the young woman and looked around the room in disbelief. "Impossible," she said to herself. "This wasn't here."

"*I am the witch you seek.*" The familiar raspy voice came into Annabelle's thoughts.

Annabelle turned around to look at the young woman. But she was replaced by a withered old woman; her once brilliant black hair was silvery grey. It was the fortune-teller from the market who had called Annabelle a traveler.

The old woman smiled, seeing that Annabelle recognized her. "I am Raj. The most powerful witch our world has left." She reached out and took Annabelle's hand in her own. "I have kept a close eye on your family."

"What do you want with my family?"

"We are family, my dear." Raj paused, picking up the fruit that had spilled out of the basket Annabelle had dropped and put it back in. "You are a descendant of my brother. One of his great, great . . . well, many-times-great grandchildren. I lose track of the years anymore."

"If it is that long ago, how are you still here?"

"I am pure magic, my dear. Immortal. My brother was, too. But he fell in love with an ordinary human, of course, and gave that all up. He chose to love someone else, and lost pieces of his magic with every child he had. My parents, like my brother, gave all their magic to us, and died as mortals. I was the only one that focused on the gift I was given, and I grew it. I did not squander it with something that will fade—love."

Raj snapped her fingers and lit the fire under the cauldron that sat in the center of the room. She pointed at each of the baskets sitting on the ground and flicked her wrist. "To the kitchen," she told them. They flew past Annabelle, her mouth open in disbelief.

"Oh child, do not act so shocked. Why do you think you are able to travel through worlds? Your father had just a sliver of magic, and it appears that was given to you. My brother's descendants' magic is so little anymore, sometimes it goes to the next generation, and sometimes it just dissolves to good luck, the magic completely dying away."

"What do you want with me?" Annabelle asked, following Raj as she walked around the room, pulling various jars off the shelves.

"The better question is, what do you want with me?" Raj asked, handing a few of the jars to Annabelle to hold as she continued pulling more off the shelves.

"My mother," Annabelle said, looking at the contents of one of the jars; it was full of spiders. She shivered and continued on: "I want to find a way to be able to see her, or some way to bring my family back together."

"Oh, yes . . . Lori," Raj said with a smile. "She was definitely the light of James's world. When his magic was strong, I must tell you, I was the one that brought him back here. Our world needed him a lot more than that wasteful world he picked did."

"You brought my father back here? You were the one that made my father abandon my mother, abandon me?!" Annabelle demanded, slamming the glass jars onto the table beside the caldron. "How could you?!"

"As I said, our world needed him more. That other world is full of death and corruption. In time, it will destroy itself."

"This is not our world! It's amazing and magical and fascinating, but my world is home with my mother, as is my father's!"

Raj smiled as she carefully lined up the jars she had pulled from the shelves. "You still have much to learn. But we don't have time for that. I needed James to fight for this world. This kingdom would not have survived the troll invasion without him. That is why I brought him back. And he was just what we needed. We had a lot of dark things coming our way, and with his leadership, we overcame it. I knew you would be searching for me soon enough." She opened one of the jars, pulled a few pine needles out and sprinkled them into the caldron.

"So, can you help me?" Annabelle asked, taking a deep breath. She needed to calm down.

"Not in the way you seek, but better," Raj said, smiling. She dumped more jars into the caldron. Feathers of a bluebird, silvery fish scales, a gold liquid, and white flower petals. She then started mixing as it boiled. Darkness crept into the room; only the fire under the caldron provided light. Raj's eyes turned cloudy white. In the same raspy voice, she said:

"Two worlds own your heart. Your parents, split apart. To make you whole, look in your soul, seek what you desire from this fire. With so much to lose, what will fate choose—united or divided."

Annabelle watched Raj mix the boiling pot. The fire cast shadows on Raj's face, giving her a tired, haggard look.

"It is finished," Raj said, reaching into the caldron. She pulled something out and wrapped it in a cloth.

Light flooded back into the room, and Raj's eyes went back to the grey-green color they had been before. Years flew off her face, and her hair returned to jet black. Raj was once again the young woman Annabelle first met. "You should get going; your friends will need you soon. This forest is not safe for those who are not magic. Your magic will protect you from certain beasts, but there still are those that are drawn to magic creatures and will want to fight you to test your powers." She paused for a minute, looking around the room. "Ah yes, here it is," Raj said, walking over to a dusty trunk. She pulled the lid open and dug through its contents. Raj pulled several things out and laid them on the table.

Annabelle walked over to look at what Raj had placed there. A small jar full of fireflies, a little wooden stick that had a vine curled around it, a skeleton key, and a lace ribbon with several turquoise stones embroidered in it. "What is this stuff?" Annabelle asked, picking up the key.

Raj smiled. "From my younger years of magic, these are what will get you through the forest and safely home." Raj put the cloth that was holding whatever she pulled from the caldron in Annabelle's hand. "And this is what will fix your traveler problem."

Annabelle opened the cloth. A long gold chain slipped out onto the table. There were several small charms dangling from the chain, but she didn't look closely at them. "I don't understand," she said, looking at Raj in confusion.

"Let me explain the rest of this quickly, you don't have much time, and I have other commitments today as well." She picked up the jar of fireflies and placed it in Annabelle's canvas bag. "This will light your way in the darkest time." She picked up the stick and also put it in the bag. "This will help protect you against your enemies."

"A stick?" Annabelle asked, raising her eyebrows.

Raj gave her a scowl and continued on. "The key will allow you passage, and this ribbon is for Rosie." Raj knelt to the ground. Rosie, who had been shivering nervously in the doorway, came trotting over to Raj. She tied the ribbon around Rosie's neck. Raj patted Rosie's head and said to her, "Now go outside, we will meet you there."

"What did that do to Rosie? And what of the chain?" Annabelle asked, picking it up and holding it in her hands. The fire's light made the gold shimmer.

"Just wait till we go outside," Raj said, smiling, "and as for the chain, wear it around your neck. When you are back to the other world, you will know what to do with it. Now, you need to go!" Raj handed Annabelle the bag and placed the gold chain around her neck. "Be safe, my great, great . . . however-distant niece. The magic runs stronger through your veins than I thought. I look forward to our future."

"Thank you, Raj, I think," Annabelle said, walking outside.

The sun was still shining brightly when she stepped outside. A huge shadow fell in the front yard of Raj's cottage. Annabelle looked up to see what was casting the shadow. It was a very large animal, with black-and-white spots and Rosie's floppy ears, a huge mane, and sharp claws and teeth. The animal stood up as she got closer, wagging its docked tail. "Rosie?" Annabelle asked, not trusting what she saw.

The beast ran over to greet Annabelle, meeting her eye to eye. She reached up to scratch it behind the ears. "Oh Rosie," she said, shaking her head. "Will she be permanently like this?" Annabelle asked Raj, who was standing in the doorway.

"Only when the collar is on," Raj said. "I would say I've made quite an improvement to her! Once it is off, she will be the floppy-eared mutt you love. Safe travels, my dear." She waved goodbye to Annabelle.

Annabelle turned back to face Rosie. She dug her fingers into Rosie's fur and laughed. "Okay, let's go, my fierce companion."

She pulled her mink shawl tightly around her shoulders and started to walk away from the cottage, back toward the woods. "Russell!" Annabelle pulled him out of her shawl pocket. She spun around to ask Raj to fix him, but the cottage was gone. There was nothing but an empty meadow left. She stood, holding Russell-the-toad in her hands, unsure of what to do now.

"If he seeks two feet to walk, send him off the hometown dock."

Annabelle smiled. "Thank you, Raj!" she said, spinning around and heading back to the forest. "We will get you fixed when we get home," she said to Russell, looking at his little scowling face before she stuck him back in her pocket.

Annabelle pushed herself to run until the little path was too rough, forcing her to slow her pace to a walk. Rosie walked clumsily behind her, stepping on the back of Annabelle's heels so frequently that she stopped to let Rosie walk in front of her, and then continued on. Surprisingly, Annabelle made it back to where the group had camped. "I can't believe we found our way back!" she said to Rosie, who trotted over to lay comfortably on the linens that had been set up for Annabelle's tent. There were times when Annabelle got lost in their own castle. The sun was setting behind the trees. She paused and looked around the area. All the tents were still there, but some had been smashed in. Their supplies were scattered around the camp. Rosie got up and sniffed at one of the tents that had been crushed, let out a low whimper, walked back to Annabelle, and sat down, shivering.

Annabelle's heart pounded heavily in her chest. She

carefully walked to each tent and looked in, just to make sure no one was left at camp. There was short black hair in several of the tents. It reminded her of Rosie's, but thicker. There were deep scratch marks on some of the nearby tree trunks. Annabelle traced her fingers down them. She pondered what could have caused this. Movement in the trees nearby interrupted her thoughts. She quickly pulled the collar Raj gave her off Rosie, shrinking the beast back into the little rat terrier. Annabelle snatched up the dog as she backed out of the clearing. She frantically climbed up a huge pine tree that overlooked the clearing; it provided her some camouflage.

Annabelle calmed her breathing and held Rosie close. She watched as five giant black wolves entered the clearing. Their yellow eyes darted around the campsite. They sniffed the tent where Rosie had been laying and scratched around it. Two huge, bald men walked into the clearing, each dropping large burlap bags to the ground with a thud. Their skin had a green tint to it and one of them had an underbite. Sharp, jagged teeth protruded from their mouths. Annabelle guessed that these were trolls. As a child she had read stories of them, but never imagined they existed in real life. Each of them carried wooden clubs and would grunt and gesture at things, not really talking.

She sat silently in the tree, watching them. It was getting dark quickly. Annabelle was trying to figure out a way to escape when one of the trolls started a fire. The other troll untied the knot on one of the burlap bags. Annabelle stared in horror as Nick tumbled out of the bag, his eyes were closed, his body limp. There was blood streaked across his forehead and down his cheek. The troll with the underbite moved to the next bag; Merry Anne was in it, her wrists and ankles tied. She looked exhausted. Annabelle's mind raced. Where was Gary?

The trolls grunted to each other some more, and eventually left Nick and Merry Anne together, propped up against the tree that Russell had sat by to keep watch. The trolls moved back to the pot, their backs to Merry Anne, Nick, and Annabelle. Annabelle strained to get a glimpse of what the trolls were putting in the pot, but she couldn't see.

She looked over at Nick and Merry Anne. Merry Anne had torn a strip from the hem of her dress and was fumbling with her bound wrists, trying to tie the strip around Nick's head. He held his bound hands up to hold it in place as Merry Anne tied it. Annabelle felt a sense of relief come over her; at least Nick was still alive!

The trolls scarfed down whatever the contents of the pot were, fighting and pushing each other to try and get the last bite. Eventually, they settled down and fell asleep, while the wolves fought to lick the remnants of the pot clean.

Silently, Annabelle watched the wolves pace around the campfire. The light cast their shadows through the trees and made their yellow eyes glow. Rosie shivered. Annabelle had hoped to save her friends while the trolls slept, but with the wolf pack there, she had no chance.

Annabelle took Russell-the-toad out of her pocket and put him on a tree branch. She wrapped Rosie in her shawl and tied it tightly to her body. Then she wrapped the strap of her pack around the tree trunk and put it back on. If she fell asleep tonight, at least she wouldn't fall out of the tree. It took some time, but the swaying of the tree in the wind slowly rocked Annabelle to sleep.

109

The Traveler

Chapter 18

Ann's alarm rang loudly in her room. She stretched and hit the snooze button. Lying in bed, she replayed the events that had just happened in her father's world. Picturing the cold, yellow eyes of the black wolves gave her goosebumps. She shook her head to get the image out of her mind, and then climbed out of bed. She needed to make the best of the day with her mom.

As she was changing her clothes, her eyes caught the glimmer of gold from the necklace around her neck. She pulled it off to examine it. It was the chain Raj had given her. She still hadn't had a chance to look over the charms that dangled from the necklace.

Ann sat at the old oak desk that was tucked in the corner of her room. She used to sit there with her father when he helped her practice her spelling words as a child. Back then, the desk was in the den. It was her father's space. Ann smiled to herself, thinking of the days when her family used to be all together. It must have pained her mother to see the empty den every day, because for a long time she kept the glass French doors closed, as if it were shut off from the rest of the house, dark and unused. Eventually her mom turned the den into a craft room, and Ann convinced her to put the desk in her room.

Shaking the memories out of her head, Ann flipped her desk lamp on and laid the necklace out under the light. The chain sparkled brightly. The center charm was a golden bird with outstretched wings. The tail feathers were split in two, entwining around each other, and at the bottom, they wrapped around a ruby cut in the shape of a heart. It was the same bird that was on her family's crest in her father's world. The other charms were smaller—a little horseshoe and a paw print. Ann held each small charm in her hand, trying to figure out what the point of this necklace was.

"Ann," her mom called, "are you awake?"

"Yes, Mom, I'll be down in a second," Ann called, turning the desk lamp off. She hustled out of her room. Skipping down the stairs, Ann put the chain back around her neck, tucking it under her shirt for safekeeping. She met her mom at the bottom of the stairs. Her mom was dressed and ready to go to town.

"I have to run some errands in town; would you like to come with me?" Ann's mom asked, pulling her purse over her shoulder.

"No," Ann said, putting on a pair of sandals. "But I'll walk you out." Ann opened the door and they stepped outside onto the porch. The clouds were dark and heavy with rain. "Be careful driving," Ann said, hugging her mom.

"Of course, sweetie," she said, kissing Ann on the head. She walked over to her car and put her purse inside.

She was just about to shut the car door when a glimmer of light caught her eye. Something was hanging from a low branch of their old oak tree. Ann's mom climbed back out of the car and walked over to the tree. She took it off the branch and studied it in her hands.

Big drops of rain started falling from the sky, and the low roar of thunder echoed off in the distance. "What did you find, Mom?" Ann asked, stepping back under the porch to avoid getting rained on.

"Let's go inside, I'll show you."

Silently, they walked to the kitchen table. Rain dripped off Ann's mom's hair and shoulders. She laid a golden chain necklace on the table, the same bird charm in the center.

Ann pulled her necklace off her neck and laid it beside the one her mom found. "Can you wait to run errands? We have a lot to talk about."

Ann's mom sat down at the table, holding the necklaces in her hands. "Our first anniversary at this house, your father hung a diamond necklace on that same branch. He always gave gifts in creative ways. For a moment I thought—well, I thought this was from him." She wiped a tear from her eye and shook her head. "I don't know why I even thought that."

"In a way mom, it is from him." Ann sat down beside her mom and held her mom's hands. "I want to tell you what has been going on, why I wasn't in bed that night you were so worried about me. But you aren't going to believe it." Ann took a deep breath and began to share her stories of her father's world, everything from the castle they lived in to the forest she was stuck in now. As they talked, the storm continued on; the rain splattered on the windows as the thunder boomed, and lightning flashed.

As Ann spoke, she tried to watch her mom's face to gauge her reaction. Her face went to a look of disbelief, worry, and ended in almost sadness.

"Ann," her mom said, exhaling heavily, "This . . . this is impossible. Are you stressed about school? Or your future? You know you can talk to me about these things."

"I know I can, Mom. And I know it sounds crazy, but I promise you it is true. Dad is there. And Aunt Ester." Ann looked at the clock. The time had flown by; it was already lunch time. "Let's go to lunch. Please don't doubt me, just trust me."

Ann's mom bit her fingernail in thought. She slowly nodded. "Lunch sounds good, sweetie. Let me grab an umbrella." Before she stood up from the table, she picked up the necklace that she found on the tree and put it around her neck, then put the other necklace on Ann. "I don't know how to process all of this, but let's keep them on, just in case."

Ann smiled. There was a chance her mom could accept all of this. They had always been close, and Ann had always been able to talk openly with her mom. She felt this would really help.

It was almost 2:00 PM before they got to Dirksen's Café for lunch. They were the only people in there. Ann and her mom ordered at the register and then sat in a little booth near the front window, silently watching the rain fall heavily onto the brick sidewalk.

"Can you tell me your story again?" Ann's mom asked, laying her napkin and silverware out.

Ann started telling her mom again, but paused when the front door opened, making the little bell ring. They watched as a little old lady walked past their booth to the front register. The old woman pulled off her handkerchief that was covering her curly silver hair. She turned and winked at Ann with her piercing grey-green eyes. It was Raj.

Ann's mouth dropped open. "Raj?" she said, her mind still in disbelief.

"Annabelle," Raj said, bowing in acknowledgment. "I am just picking up a sandwich to go," Raj said to the clerk at the counter, who took her money and handed her a sandwich in a paper bag. Raj turned back to Ann. "Bundle up, worlds tend to share the same weather." And with that, she slipped out the door and was gone.

"Raj, the witch?" Ann's mom asked, shaking her head. "I cannot believe this."

Ann smiled and said, "It's a whole new world, Mom."

They ate their lunch, although neither of them seemed to have much of an appetite. Ann was too excited to share her stories with her mom, and her mom already had too much to digest before she even started eating lunch. By the time they left the café, they had spent two hours there. The sun was peeking through the clouds, and the rain had come to a halt.

The rest of the day Ann and her mom spent working with Lucy and weeding the garden. The wind picked up and the rain clouds loomed over them once again, forcing them to go into the house for the night.

Both Ann and her mom went to their rooms to put on pajamas, their hair drenched from the rain.

They met back in the living room and sat on the couch, eventually turning on the television. Her mom reached over and held Ann's hand, smiling comfortingly at her. Ann felt like a weight had been lifted off her shoulders. She finally had told her mom everything.

In a short couple of hours, both Ann and her mom fell asleep on the couch.

Chapter 19

Annabelle woke up in the evergreen tree, grasping for branches as she felt the tree swaying from side to side from the wind. The branches were slick with rain. Her hands landed on someone else's arm—her mother's.

Annabelle's mom was clinging to the evergreen tree, a look of shock plastered on her face. Annabelle helped her to a sturdy branch, and held her finger to her lips, motioning her to be silent. Annabelle pointed down to the trolls in the clearing.

The rain was beating down on the sleeping trolls, who did not even seem to notice it. Merry Anne and Nick were huddled under a tree. They looked exhausted. Annabelle searched the clearing for the wolves; they were nowhere to be found.

Annabelle carefully untied the pack from the tree's branches and put it back over her shoulders. She tucked Russell-the-toad carefully in her shawl pocket. Aunt Ester's mink fur shawl would never look nice again. She felt a sense of guilt grow in the pit of her stomach. Aunt Ester always wore this on important occasions.

Rosie shivered nervously as Annabelle tucked her

under her arm. She motioned to her mom that she was going to go down the tree and try and help Merry Anne and Nick. She gestured for her mom to stay in the tree.

Her mom shook her head. "NO."

Annabelle nodded and started climbing down the tree. Her mom followed her. When they got to the bottom of the tree, Annabelle looked over at her mom. She had their cat, Cleo, tucked under her arm. Annabelle had to cover her mouth to keep from laughing out loud. Why on earth was Cleo here?

Annabelle's mom shrugged her shoulders and put Cleo down in the wet grass. Cleo looked up in annoyance. She was not impressed by the rain, or by being outside. Rosie excitedly sniffed Cleo, who put her ears flat back on her head as a warning for Rosie to back off.

They inched closer to the clearing when they heard branches rustling behind them. Annabelle grabbed her mom's arm to move her away when she caught sight of Lucy, nervously sniffing the air. Her ears were pointing forward, listening curiously. Annabelle's mom turned to look at Annabelle, whose mouth was open in confusion. How was it possible that her mom, her cat, and her horse from her other world were in this world?

She shook off her thoughts and turned back toward the clearing. She had to hurry up and save Nick and Merry Anne, find Gary and get away from the trolls and wolves! The rain would help cover any noise as the trolls slept, and it should help cover their tracks if they got away before the wolves got back. The morning sun was swallowed up by the black storm clouds.

As they got to the clearing, Annabelle stopped, stretching her arms out to stop her mom or Lucy from moving forward. The trolls were stirring. She looked past them to Nick and Merry Anne. Gary was there, untying them!

Gary paused and looked up. He saw Annabelle. He signaled her to go around the clearing, through the woods. He needed help. Quickly, Annabelle and her mom snuck through the woods. Cleo, Rosie, and Lucy stayed close behind them.

Gary had managed to pull Nick and Merry Anne a little way out of the clearing by the time Annabelle got to him. He was redressing Nick's gash on his head as Merry Anne finished untying their ankles. Annabelle and her mother knelt down beside them in the mud, the rain beating down on the group.

A roar from one of the trolls made Annabelle jump. "They're up," Gary whispered, his eyes darting around the group. "Nick and Merry Anne won't be moving too quickly, and the trolls ate two of our horses. The third, Merry Anne's horse, ran off." Gary stood up, pulling his bow from his back. "I will buy us some time, if you can get those two on that horse." He gestured toward Lucy.

"Let me help you," Annabelle said, standing up. "I can buy us more time, too."

"No, Princess. It's my job to protect you. Your father would not appreciate you battling trolls!" Gary said, taking a step toward the clearing. The trees were rustling, and the angry growls of the trolls were getting closer. "Hurry now! They're coming!" Gary hissed, pushing Nick and Merry Anne up onto the horse. He then headed closer to the clearing, disappearing from their view.

Terror reflected in her mom's eyes. Her hands were shaking, and her skin was pale. There was no way they were going to be able to run through the forest. Annabelle didn't even know which way to go!

Annabelle threw her pack off her shoulder. She grabbed the collar Raj gave her out of the bag and put it on Rosie. As she was pulling her hand out of the bag, she brushed against the stick Raj had given her. *"This will help protect you against your enemies."* Raj's words echoed in her head.

"But it's a stick . . . ," Annabelle said to herself, pulling it out of her bag. "A stick with a vine on it. I must be crazy." She pushed her mom onto Rosie-the-beast's back, throwing Cleo up to her. "Follow Merry Anne, I will meet up with you soon."

Annabelle walked over and looked to Merry Anne, who nodded reassuringly. She grabbed Nick's hand and held it firmly, studying his face. He was pale and shivering.

Her mother was barely functioning, she was in such shock. Clutching Rosie's mane, she took a shallow breath. She pleaded, "Ann, please don't go."

But Annabelle was already headed toward the clearing, her pack slung over her shoulder and the little stick with the vine wrapped around it clutched in her hands.

By the time Annabelle reached Gary, the wolves had found the trolls. The wolves were lined up in front of the two trolls, saliva dripping from their mouths in anticipation of a fight. They crinkled up their lips to show their sharp teeth, low growls coming from their throats. The troll with an underbite was holding his arm, one of Gary's arrows was sticking out of it. Dark-blue blood was running down from the wound, falling from his elbow to the mud below.

"Annabelle!" Gary shouted, "I said stay back!"

"I can't let you do this alone," Annabelle said, shocked at her own bravery. In her mom's world, she didn't even like giving speeches in front of her class. And now, she is about to take on a wolf pack and two giant trolls.

One of the wolves advanced, lunging at Annabelle. Gary shot it with one of his arrows. The wolf let out a howl as it retreated to the pack, the arrow sticking out of its shoulder.

The unharmed troll grunted an order to the wolves. They all inched forward anxiously.

Gary shot another arrow into the group; this one was a fatal shot to one of the wolves. It let out a yelp as it collapsed to the ground.

"Enough!" Annabelle shouted, taking a step forward. She pointed the stick at the trolls. "Stop!" she cried.

At first, nothing happened. Silence fell among the wolves as they stared apprehensively at the stick.

Annabelle felt her skin grow hot. Her veins burned, as if they were on fire. Vines flooded out from the stick and slithered up from the ground. The vines wrapped themselves around the trolls, twisting from the ground up to their legs to their waists.

The trolls grunted in anger, using their clubs to fight off the vines. But it was wasted effort. The vines grew thicker and overwhelmed the trolls. Soon they climbed up the trolls' arms and shoulders until the trolls were completely immobile.

The wolves screamed in fear of the magic. The pack scattered into the forest, leaving only the bound trolls and the one dead wolf.

Gary looked over to Annabelle, raising his eyebrows in surprise. "Magic?" He put his bow back over his shoulder. "How is it possible?"

Annabelle tucked the stick back in her pack. She pulled Russell out of her shawl. "The witch we were looking for found us. This little toad is Russell."

Gary chuckled. "It looks just like Russell. I wonder if it is the same witch that once turned him into a lizard." He took Russell from Annabelle. "Oh Russell, you make a very handsome toad."

"The witch said to put him in water off the dock at home. That will make him human again." Annabelle took Russell from Gary, putting him back in her pocket.

"I saw Lace's tracks when I was headed this way. I think she has been circling the camp looking for Merry Anne. If we could find her, we can use her to catch up with the others—hopefully before the wolves get their courage back." Gary led them out of the clearing. He knelt down to study Lace's tracks.

Annabelle heard the nicker of a horse; she looked around and saw Lace standing in the brush nearby. "Over there," Annabelle said, pointing.

Gary walked over and untangled her reins from the brush. "She's lucky trolls don't have the best vision. She probably would have been their next meal, or Nick and Merry Anne. When I woke up to take over watch from Russell, I realized you were gone. I looked around a bit to find you when the trolls showed up. The troll I shot in the arm hit Nick over the head and tied him and Merry Anne up." He paused to climb onto Lace, pulling Annabelle up after him. "I kept watch for the right time to try and free them."

"The witch gave me the ability to put my mom in this world," Annabelle said, brushing her wet hair from her face. "My mom is terrified."

Gary laughed as he flicked the reins. "It was quite the start to this world."

"I suppose you're right," Annabelle said, straining to look through the trees and the rain to find her mom, Nick, and Merry Anne.

It didn't take long for Gary and Annabelle to catch up. Rosie was still very clumsy in her big body, and the rain made it hard to see to navigate. They rode at a trot, trying to get a good distance between the trolls and themselves.

When the pace slowed, and the horses and Rosie were breathing hard, the group stopped for a break. Annabelle guessed it was close to noon. She helped her mom down and pulled Rosie's collar off. They took shelter from the rain in a small cave opening that was just a short distance from the path they were traveling on.

Gary led the group into the cave. It opened up into a large room. It was very dark, but dry. Annabelle pulled the glass jar of fireflies out of her pack. Somehow, the fireflies managed to illuminate the entire cave. She smiled at Raj's magic. The roots from the trees above hung down from the top of the cave, casting shadows on the walls. Quietly, the group all sat together. Annabelle introduced her mother to Gary, Nick, and Merry Anne. Her mom still looked shook up, but the color was coming back to her face.

"Everything is too wet to make a fire," Gary said, looking around the cave for sticks. "I don't see anything in here. If we don't get dried off, we risk illness. Nick's cut needs addressing, too. Trolls have toxins on their clubs. I packed it with the herbs Merry Anne had with her, but that won't be enough."

The group sat in silence, listening to the rain outside. Thunder and lightning filled the sky. Merry Anne broke the silence: "It might be best if we spend the night here."

Annabelle looked at Nick. Dark circles hung below his eyes. His skin was pale and yellowed in the glow of the fireflies. Nick's eyes met hers. "We aren't far enough away from the wolves and trolls. They will track us here, especially when the horses are standing right outside. The trolls will smell them."

"He's right," Merry Anne said, standing up. "I will send Lace home. She knows the way. We can tie the other horse to her; Lace will keep them safe."

Gary nodded in approval. "It will make our journey home much longer. But we will have a better chance if the trolls follow their tracks instead of ours." Gary followed Merry Anne out of the cave into the rain to help her tie the two horses together.

"Some of my clothes that were in my pack didn't get wet; we can dry off with them," Annabelle said, digging through her bag. She pulled out the skeleton key and studied it. Everything Raj had given her had made sense so far, but what did this one mean? She handed her mother her lilac-colored dress. She took it and walked deeper into the cave to take her wet clothes off and put the dry ones on.

Nick smiled a tired smile. "I don't imagine I will look as nice in a dress as you do, Annabelle."

"Oh, I have a blue one that would bring out the color of your eyes beautifully."

Nick laughed, putting his hand on hers. "Back at the

clearing, when you disappeared—I was truly worried about you."

"I'm sorry, Nick. I felt terrible for abandoning the group." Annabelle paused while her mom, Gary, and Merry Anne came back to sit beside them. They all accepted some clothes from her pack to dry off with or change into.

After everyone had settled in, Annabelle cleared her throat. "I want to tell you what became of me when you guys were all battling trolls." Before she began, she rationed out the small amount of food she had in her pack to each person in the group, tossing a small piece each to Rosie and Cleo.

The group sat closely together as Annabelle told her story. They talked until dark, sharing stories with each other, learning more about Annabelle and her mom's world, and scavenging for food and firewood. The rain turned to hail as it pounded against the mouth of the cave, forcing the group to move deeper into the cave. The group slowly started to fall asleep huddled together, Gary sitting up keeping watch.

"Annabelle!" Nick whispered, shaking her shoulder.

Annabelle sat up, feeling the ground vibrate beneath her. "What was that?" she asked, grabbing her mother's hand.

"The trolls, they found us! They are beating down the cave entrance," Gary said, pulling Merry Anne to her feet. "Hurry and put that light away, we need to move deeper into the cave. I think there should be a way out."

Quickly, the group moved silently farther into the cave single file, led by Gary, with Cleo and Rosie closely at their heels.

Annabelle strained her eyes to see. The darkness engulfed them after she put her firefly jar away. The full moon outside did not penetrate far enough into the cave to help her see anything. Annabelle struggled to keep her footing; the rocky floor of the cave caused her to stumble several times. She held tightly onto her mom, who was following behind her. As exhausted as she was, the roars and grunts of the trolls kept her moving forward.

The group came to a fork in the cave tunnels, branching off in four directions. Rosie sniffed the air nervously as they picked the far-right tunnel to go through. It seemed like hours as they turned and twisted through the caves. They paused to listen for the trolls, only hearing the echoing sound of the rain.

The group sat down to rest their feet. "What do we do now?" Annabelle asked, rubbing her feet. They were sore; her ankles were scuffed and rubbed raw from the rocky, jagged cave floor.

"There will be a way out," Gary said, looking around the cave. "Dwarves built these caves long ago. They always made several exits."

"Dwarves?" Annabelle's mom asked, still trying to comprehend everything that had happened to her.

Merry Anne smiled sadly. "Yes, one of the most kindhearted beings that ever walked in our world. They are all gone now. The only things that live in these caves anymore are magical creatures in danger of going extinct with the dwarves."

"What other creatures?" Annabelle's mom asked before Annabelle was able to.

"Pixies mostly—" Nick was cut off, there was a crushing sound and the wall beside the group crumpled in. In front of them stood the troll with an underbite, Gary's arrow still sticking out of its arm.

"What do we do now?!" Annabelle cried.

"We will have to fight," Gary said, reaching to grab his bow.

"We can't fight like this," Merry Anne said. "Everyone is exhausted. And we can't keep running!"

Annabelle pulled the skeleton key out of her bag and held it in the air. Somehow, even in the darkness, the silver key glowed. "WE WANT TO GO HOME!" Annabelle yelled, closing her eyes tightly.

Chapter 20

Ann stretched, waking up slowly. Her head was in a fog as she sat up and looked around. Her mind raced. She replayed the events of what had happened in her father's world. She reached out and touched a strand of her mother's hair, brushing it away from her face. It was still damp. Her cheeks were pale, and she was shivering. Ann sat up and climbed off the couch to grab a blanket for her mom when she tripped over something big on the floor, landing hard on her back.

She closed her eyes for a minute, trying to clear her head. Ann opened her eyes and rolled over to come face-to-face with Nick. Shocked, she stood up. Their entire traveling group that was just huddled in a cave in her father's world was now in her living room with her mom! Nick, Merry Anne, Gary, Russell-the-toad, Rosie, and Cleo.

The group all looked to Ann as she studied their surprised faces. She took a deep breath and said, "Well, at least the troll didn't come with us."

"What do we do now?" her mom asked, standing up

and putting her hand on Ann's shoulder.

"Let's get Nick cleaned up," Ann said, touching the dried blood on his cheek.

"I think we have some antibiotics in the medicine cabinet to help that gash," her mom said, helping Nick to his feet. Gary took Nick's arm and led him up the stairs, following Ann's mom to the bathroom. Merry Anne trailed closely behind, pausing to touch the light switch in wonder.

Ann looked down to see Russell-the-toad sitting in her lap. She smiled, picking him up in her hands and carrying him over to the laptop computer that was sitting on the coffee table. "Well, Russell, I can show you what the internet is now." She placed him beside the computer and turned it on.

After a while, the group came back down the stairs, all sticking very closely together, walking carefully through the house as if something was going to jump out and attack them. Ann looked closely at Nick. There was some color coming back in his face; his wound was properly dressed, and his face had been cleaned up.

"Their clothes were all soaked, so I lent Gary and Nick some of your dad's clothes," Ann's mom said, sitting down beside Ann. "Merry Anne and I are practically the same size," she said, smiling at Ann.

"Thank you for your hospitality," Merry Anne said, walking over to Ann's mother. "I have never worn jeans before—they are amazing!"

Ann studied the group. They looked so different in her world's clothing. Someone could pass by them on the street and have no idea they were from a completely different world.

"I think Nick will be fine with some rest. . . . Your world has some crazy medicine," Gary said, helping Nick to sit on the couch.

"What do we do now?" Ann asked, looking around the group.

"The best place to start would be some tea and hot food," Ann's mom said, heading to the kitchen. "I will start cooking something up; it's a good thing we got groceries."

"I would be happy to assist you. On our trip to the forest Annabelle told us about how your world cooks things. I would love to see it in person," Merry Anne said, joining Ann's mother. Rosie must have heard the word "food," because she was quick to follow them.

Gary, Nick, and Ann sat in silence in the living room. Cleo sat on the floor, still attempting to lick her fur dry. Ann studied Nick's face. He really did look like he was feeling better than he had in the cave.

"We will have to figure out a way back," Gary said, breaking the silence. "And that may mean facing the trolls."

Nick nodded in agreement. "Annabelle said she traveled through the worlds when she fell asleep. So, we may have some time to waste. Maybe we can explore this world for the day." He smiled at Ann, a glimmer of excitement in his eyes.

Ann felt butterflies in her stomach. She had been so worried about her journey; she forgot to appreciate how handsome Nick was. For the first time in a while, she felt hopeful.

They talked about plans for when they got back to her dad's world, but soon the smell of food cooking pulled the group into the kitchen. As they walked in, Merry Anne was opening and closing the fridge door, looking around every inch of the kitchen.

"Whatever you are cooking, it smells amazing," Gary said, sitting down at the table.

"Thank you," Ann's mom said, smiling with pride. "James always loved my cooking, too. Merry Anne helped me spice the pork chops. I had never thought to make it this way." She placed the pork on the table, along with broccoli from the garden, pasta salad, garlic bread, and the teapot.

Everyone sat down, watching the warm steam roll off the food. Ann started passing the bowls of food, and everyone filled their plates. There wasn't much talking while people ate, just the pleasant silence and feeling of relief to be safe and dry.

The food disappeared quickly as everyone ate their fill. Ann cleared the plates from the table, but everyone remained seated, drinking their tea.

After Nick was done eating, he was back to his cheerful self. He joked with Gary and talked with Ann's mom. Whatever medicine Ann's mom and Merry Anne gave him, it must have done the trick.

"Mom, I was thinking. . . . Could I show them more of our world? Uptown? Maybe take them to the movies?"

Ann's mom smiled. "Of course, if everyone is up to it. I would like to get some things done around here."

"If it's okay with you, I would like to stay here, too," Merry Anne said, stretching her arms. "I have had enough excitement for a little while, and that couch was very comfortable."

"Our beds are even better," Ann's mother said,

standing up. "Follow me; you can sleep in Ann's room. I think I could use a nap, too."

Gary, Nick, and Ann climbed into her little red pickup truck to go to town. Gary and Nick were amazed at vehicles; they truly didn't need a horse to pull them. The rest of the day flew by. She took them to the mall and to see the latest action movie that was showing in the theater. They blended in perfectly, except for the few times Gary and Nick jumped up to fight whatever popped out at them in the 3D movie.

When Ann pulled the pickup back home under the old oak tree, the sun was setting. She looked down at Russell-the-toad, who was sitting on the dash of the truck. "Do you think he will remember all of this?" she asked, picking him up.

"I still hear him complain about his life as a lizard, so I am sure we will hear about this, too," Gary said with a smile.

Ann led the group back to the house but stopped short of the front door. Someone was sitting on the porch, in her mom's rocking chair. She walked over to get a closer look. It was Raj, cupping a mug of warm peppermint tea. She had a worried look on her face.

"Raj?" Ann asked in surprise.

"Annabelle. How did this happen?" she said, gesturing to Nick and Gary. "Their feet were not meant to stand in this world."

"It was the key you gave me. It brought us all here."

"No, little Princess," Raj said, shaking her head. "There was not enough magic in that key. It was made for one traveler."

"I held it up and then we ended up here," Ann replied,

sitting in the chair next to Raj.

"She yelled, 'I want to go home,' as well," Nick said, taking Russell-the-toad out of Ann's hands. Then, respectfully, Gary and Nick went inside the house to give them some privacy.

Raj pursed her lips together, as she was deep in thought. "Impossible," she said, mostly to herself. "Give me your hand," Raj said to Ann, holding her wrinkled hand out to Ann.

Ann reached her hand out to Raj. Raj held it tightly as her eyes fogged over, turning completely white. Ann waited anxiously, trying to study Raj's face.

Slowly, Raj's grip loosened and the grey-green color in her eyes returned. She stood up, dropping Ann's hand. "My dear, your life is so much more than I even imagined. Your magic—I don't even believe it. Impossible." Raj stepped off the porch, almost stumbling away from Ann.

"What do you mean? Raj, wait!" Ann called watching Raj walk past the oak tree. She hopped off the porch and followed after her.

As Ann got past the tree, Raj was nowhere to be found. "What do you mean?" Ann asked again, looking around.

"My brother's magic is in your heart, you will give our world a new start," echoed in Ann's ears as she walked back into the house.

Ann's mom had made up beds for everyone in the living room. There were blankets and pillows neatly placed around the floor and couches. Everyone was talking in the living room. Ann stood in the hall for a moment, watching the happy group.

"Merry Anne thought it might be best if we all slept in

the same room," Nick said as he caught sight of Ann. "Just to be safe; we don't want to risk anyone not getting to go back to our world. Although, she said the beds here were pretty amazing." He smiled, his beautiful blue eyes looking into Ann's.

"That sounds good," Ann said, smiling at Nick. "Mom, could I talk to you in the kitchen for a second?"

Ann and her mom stood by the kitchen sink. "Is everything okay?" her mom asked, a worried look on her face.

"Yes, but I wanted to ask you. . . . Are you ready to go back to that other world? Do you even want to, or would you rather be here?"

"Wherever you go, I want to go, too," she said, hugging her daughter closely. "You are my world, sweetie."

"Thank you, Mom," Ann said, hugging her mom back. "Let's go to bed."

It took a while for everyone to get calmed down to go to sleep; they were excitedly recapping the day. Rosie sighed and snuggled in closely to Ann, burying herself against Ann's back. Cleo frowned in annoyance, as that was her usual spot. Slowly, the group settled in for the night.

Chapter 21

Cold water dripped off the cave walls and onto Annabelle's head. Before she opened her eyes, she listened to the roaring thunder. The storm had carried on through the night and was still raging outside this morning. Carefully, she sat up and looked around. They had made it back to the cave. The walls were crumbled down around them; deep scratches were carved into the broken walls from the trolls' clubs. As Ann's eyes adjusted to the dark, she slowly made out the silhouettes of the two trolls, hunched together against a rock across the room from the group. The trolls were asleep. Their heavy breathing echoed off the broken walls and through the cave.

Nick quietly touched Annabelle's shoulder, breaking her focus on the trolls. He led her out of the room. The rest of the group was already waiting there for her. Even in the dimly lit room she could make out the nervous looks plastered on their faces.

"We are all here," Gary whispered to Annabelle, "even your mom." He paused, listening for the snoring of the trolls. "But we have to get far away from here. Even the wolves are back. Our disappearance must have confused the trolls. It looks like they tore this cave to pieces trying to find us. But we are on the right track to finding a way out, as long as we keep following the path the water is draining to. There will be a way out."

Annabelle nodded, looking at Merry Anne. She was holding Cleo in her arms. She must have taken pity on the cat, who still did not look very happy to be back in the cave.

Silently, the group pushed on. Water had pooled on the ground of the uneven cave floor. It wasn't long until Annabelle's feet were cold and pruned from stepping in the puddles.

For what seemed like hours, the group walked through the cave. Annabelle's eyes were tired. There were parts of the cave where she could see a small distance in front of her, but for the most part, eyes open or closed, all she saw was the darkness swallowing her. She almost felt claustrophobic, completely engulfed in the black emptiness of the cave.

The group followed closely together, their eyes searching the endless black of the cave for any hint of light. The increasingly loud sound of running water off the walls filled their ears, eventually drowning out the thunder outside.

Abruptly, everyone stopped. It was so sudden that Annabelle ran into the person in front of her. She tried to see what was going on, but it was too dark. Annabelle dug through her bag and pulled out the jar of fireflies. The jar illuminated the cave. She held it out in front of her to investigate what the holdup was. Nick and Gary were kneeling on the ground, peering over the broken path that turned into a small waterfall, cascading down into a lake, still inside the cave.

Gary and Nick looked grimly at each other. "It looks like we may be getting wet again," Gary said, standing up. "The water is pooling here. I can almost guarantee there is a way out down there. Can everyone swim?"

Annabelle looked from one face to another; everyone in the group nodded nervously.

Merry Anne tucked Cleo and Rosie into Annabelle's pack. "I can carry this," she said, starting to pull the strap off Annabelle's shoulder.

"No, I've got it," Annabelle said, wanting the weight of Rosie as reassurance to keep her going.

Gary and Nick were the first to step off the ledge, splashing into the water below. Merry Anne quickly followed. Annabelle lowered the pack to Nick, who held Cleo and Rosie above his head and safely dry as he treaded water. Annabelle's mom took her hand. Squeezing it reassuringly, they both jumped in together.

The cold water took Annabelle by surprise. She gasped, trying to take in more air. The water was deep. Annabelle strained to touch the bottom, but she was far from reaching. Treading water, the group circled together.

"Pull those fireflies out again, Annabelle," Gary said, swimming up to her. "I will dive under and look for an exit. The tunnel continues from here. I will find the path that takes us out, and then come back for all of you. I would just like some light." As he took the jar out of her hands, the light went out, and the group was swallowed up by darkness again.

Annabelle reached out and took the jar back.

Immediately, the jar lit the cave once again.

Gary shook his head. "I—I guess I should have figured it wouldn't work for me," he said. "But still, I will find a way out."

"No," Annabelle said, not even realizing what words were coming out of her mouth. "It has to be me."

"NO," her mom said, putting her hand on her daughter's shoulder. "You will not."

The group nodded in agreement. "No person here will let that happen," Nick said, looking sternly at Annabelle.

"We don't have a choice. With the amount of water that is flooding in, we will soon have too much water. We would either need to go back and face the trolls and wolves, or drown," Annabelle said. "I can do this." In her mind, Annabelle was wondering what the heck she was thinking!

The group knew she was right. Helplessly, they watched her take a deep breath and dive under the water.

Annabelle clutched the jar of fireflies in her hand as she swam down into one of the tunnels. The water pushed her forward, the current was strong. In school, Annabelle was a strong swimmer. She felt comfortable holding her breath underwater.

As she swam, her mind wandered to her mom. She was proud of her mom for jumping into the water. In the past, she had teased her often about not knowing how to swim. Her dad had taken her mom on a cruise, and several times they went on romantic vacations to tropical far away beaches. In all the photos they had displayed on the mantle of their adventures, both her mom and dad stood, ankle deep in the water with nervous smiles on their faces. It wasn't until her dad disappeared that

Annabelle was able to convince her mom to learn how to swim.

Her lungs started to burn now, and she started to doubt her choice of a tunnel. There was no air pocket above the water in the small tunnel to fill her lungs with. She turned to go back, but already knew she would not make it all the way there. How could she be so stupid? She was not an adventurer. She was not brave like Gary or clever like Nick. She didn't know how to pick a tunnel like Merry Anne could have; she just swam into one without even processing that it could be the wrong choice.

"*Trust yourself,*" echoed into her head.

"How can I?" she thought, her lungs burning for air, her muscles screaming as her body craved one deep breath of oxygen.

"*The magic in your blood will get you out of the flood.*"

Annabelle turned around again. She wasn't sure which way she was facing now, back toward the group or still headed farther away. She let the current push her forward. Black spotty flashes scattered across her vision as she was starting to faint from lack of oxygen. She squeezed her eyes shut and tried to clear her head. "I can do this," she thought. Suddenly, words flooded into her mind: "Air surround me, get me through; circle around me and save my crew."

The pressure of the current broke. Annabelle could feel water dripping from her hair down the back of her neck and onto her clothes. She opened her eyes to try and comprehend this. She was standing on the slimy rock ground of the little tunnel, gulping in damp air. Water was rushing around her, but she was not getting wet. Annabelle was enclosed in an air bubble. She looked at her hands, pruned from being in the water so long. The water had washed away her jar of fireflies. Annabelle frowned sadly. She had hoped to give that back to Raj someday.

Annabelle continued on; the sound of the water was deafening around her, her heart pounded. Soon the tunnel opened. She looked above her and saw sunlight streaming through the water. She was right! She picked the right tunnel! She laughed in excitement. Quickly, Annabelle ran back through the tunnel to get the rest of her group.

Halfway back through the tunnel, Annabelle saw someone swimming toward her. She squinted, trying to see through the rushing water. It was Gary. She watched as he carefully swam, using his hands to feel out in front of him, searching through the darkness.

Quickly, Annabelle increased her pace. She stumbled as her feet slipped on the moss-covered tunnel. She reached out and grabbed Gary's arm. Annabelle watched in amazement as the little air bubble around her swirled around Gary's arm, around his head, and eventually grew to surround his whole body as well.

"Annabelle!" Gary exclaimed, gasping for air. "You're okay! We were starting to worry—you had been gone far too long." Gary leaned down to touch the rock beneath his feet. He paused for a moment, picking up one of the rocks on the cave floor. "How are you doing this?"

Annabelle smiled. "I'm really not sure!"

"We must get back to the group; this is amazing! Is it one of the witch's tricks?" Gary asked.

"Her name is Raj, and maybe," Annabelle said, following behind Gary through the tunnel. She kept her hand firmly on his arm as they walked, unsure if the magic would continue to cover him if they weren't touching.

When Gary and Annabelle reached the group, Gary turned back to Annabelle. "I will have the group swim down to you. Let's make sure everyone can breathe in this bubble underwater with you before we get too far. No normal person will be able to hold their breath long enough to swim through that entire tunnel."

Annabelle nodded and watched Gary swim back to the surface. It wasn't long before her mom was underwater and linking arms with her. The air bubbles twirled around her mom. Merry Ann linked arms with Annabelle's mom before she was even completely surrounded by the air, and soon the entire group was standing at the bottom of the tunnel, arm in arm, comfortably breathing air.

"This is amazing!" Nick exclaimed, looking closely at the water rushing completely around them.

Annabelle smiled, feeling proud of this ability. They walked through the dim tunnel, listening to the water rush around them. Annabelle's veins started to burn like fire. She could feel her blood pumping through them. Her heart was pounding louder in her ears. Annabelle almost felt faint, but she pressed on. If she was going to get everyone through safely, she would need to hurry.

"You are glowing, Ann!" Her mom exclaimed.

Annabelle looked back to see the terrified look on her mother's face. She paused and looked down at herself. Her veins were glowing, a bright gold. She could see it in her hands and arms, and on her chest. She took a deep breath. "Let's hurry," Annabelle said, starting to run through the tunnel, holding her mom's hand tightly. "Everyone, hang on, don't let go!"

The group sped through the tunnel. Annabelle felt as

if her arm might be pulled from its socket as she was jolted and jerked around as people in the line would stumble on the rocks or slip on the moss on the cave floor, but she held tightly to her mother.

She came to a stop when they reached the opening, where the rays of sunlight were pushing their way through the water to reach the rocky bottom. "We are here," she said, smiling with relief.

As the group unlinked arms and swam to the surface, Annabelle watched the air bubbles disperse, slowly floating to the surface. She felt the water flow back over her feet, and soon she was engulfed in water again. She weakly swam toward the sunlight. When she broke through the water's surface, Nick's arm was around her, making sure to keep her head above water.

The afternoon sun was almost blinding as the group stumbled to the shore. Exhausted, Annabelle leaned against a twisted, dying tree that shaded the water. She slid her way down the trunk until she was sitting on the rocky shore.

Her mother sat down beside her, holding Annabelle's hand. The rest of the group stood closely beside them. Gary's eyes darted around the tree line, searching for any sign of danger.

"We can't linger much longer," Gary said after a few minutes, leaning down to take Annabelle's hand and help her to her feet. "I'm sorry we won't have time for lunch. We have stirred up enough of the creatures here; who knows what else will find us."

Annabelle sighed. She took her pack back from Nick, let Rosie and Cleo out, and then took Gary's hand to stand up, her legs shaking beneath her. Her mom brushed

Annabelle's wet hair away from her face. Together they followed Gary back into the woods.

The group walked through the dense woods single file. There was no trail to follow, and the limbs of the trees and bushes grabbed onto them as they tried to push through. The dry branches cracked and snapped noisily as they broke away to let the group pass. The sun was setting quickly, but the group pressed on.

Annabelle was tired and hungry. She looked behind her at her mother. Her mom had dark circles under her eyes. Even Rosie, who was sticking close to Annabelle, looked worn out.

Gary stopped the group, listening intently. He pointed up ahead. Annabelle could see a campfire. The group inched closer for a better look, carefully stepping through the woods now, trying not to make noise. Gary stopped beside a tall pine tree, the group following behind him, hiding themselves in the thick branches.

Annabelle peered over one of the branches to see what was ahead. A small clearing sat in the woods, with a fire blazing in the center of it. Several small covered wagons were circled around the fire. A group of people outside one of the wagons was laughing among themselves as they hung wet clothes on a line to dry.

"Gypsies," Nick whispered to Annabelle.

One of the wooden wagons had various-sized cages hanging on the outside of it. Annabelle squinted, trying to see what the cages contained, but with no luck.

"AHEM." Someone behind the group noisily cleared his throat.

Annabelle turned around to see a thin, tall man. He was dressed in vibrant red-and-purple linens. His jet-black hair was long and wild.

"It seems we have some unexpected visitors tonight," the man said, twirling his beard in his fingers as he walked up closer to the group. "We are a very private traveling party, and don't appreciate people who just drop in on us." He stopped in front of the pine tree, closest to Nick.

Gary and Nick stepped out of the branches of the pine tree. "I apologize," Gary said, stepping toward the man. "My name is Gary. Our group was just trying to find a path back home."

The man leaned to the left, peering past Gary and Nick into the pine tree's branches at Annabelle, her mom, and Merry Anne. "I see," he said slowly. "Well, it is getting dangerously dark to be traveling." He set his gaze back on Nick and Gary. "And our dinner is almost ready. You must join us."

Gary and Nick looked at each other hesitantly. They turned and motioned for the rest of the group to come out of the trees.

Annabelle was nervous. She could sense the tension Gary and Nick were feeling toward the Gypsy man. As a child, she would sneak into her father's library and read about the Gypsies. In her father's books they worshiped magic and were well known for being con artists. Their free-spirited personalities and lack of roots to any specific place fascinated Annabelle. Her family's roots ran deep; she almost felt suffocated.

The group followed the man into the clearing. As they walked toward the center of the wagons, near the fire, the Gypsies that had been hanging laundry quieted their conversation and stared curiously at Annabelle's group.

"My name is Anton," the man said, bowing.

"Thank you for your hospitality, Anton," Gary said, bowing as well.

"The woods are no place for the princess," Anton said, stepping boldly in front of Annabelle. He took her hand in his and kissed it. His beard was scratchy and rough on Annabelle's hand. Annabelle fought the urge to pull her hand away. Something about him made her skin crawl. "I had heard rumors that she was out of the castle, but to be in the Enchanted Forest?"

"Yes," Gary said, stepping in between Anton and Annabelle. "She is just touring parts of her father's kingdom."

Anton raised his eyebrows in suspicion. "Curious," he said tartly. He turned toward the other Gypsies, who had now all gathered around Annabelle's traveling group. They carried various pots and pans, and several dead rabbits and vegetables. Anton addressed the Gypsy group, "Everyone: Princess Annabelle and her traveling party. They will be joining us tonight." He then turned toward Annabelle's group. "Please, sit," he said, gesturing toward one of the large wooden logs that was lying on its side, next to the fire.

Annabelle studied the Gypsy group. There was one older woman sitting in a chair beside one of the covered wagons. Her skin was brown and leathery. The breeze blew her curly grey-and-black hair. This older woman was attentively watching three younger girls prepare the meal over the fire.

At first, the young girls were quietly cooking, taking curious glances at Annabelle and the rest of her group. By the time the mouthwatering smell of the cooked rabbit reached Annabelle, the three girls were talking happily among themselves.

There was a group of men standing back from the fire. They were talking quietly, pausing off and on to look over at Annabelle and the rest of her traveling group. Anton was part of that conversation.

"It's going to be okay," Nick said, leaning over and whispering to Annabelle. "We just have to do what they say. Gypsies can have quite a temper. We don't want to rustle anyone's feathers here."

Annabelle nervously bit the inside of her cheek. She could cut the tension surrounding them with a knife. The only member of her group that seemed to be comfortable was Rosie, who was playfully chasing blue and purple scarves that two of the young Gypsy boys were making twirl in the wind toward her.

Anton came and sat down beside Nick. "Let's eat!" he said, raising his arms toward one of the young Gypsies. She brought each person a little wooden bowl full of vegetables and rabbit meat.

"Thank you," Annabelle said, smiling at the young Gypsy.

As dinner was finishing up, an old Gypsy man holding a guitar sat beside Nick. Softly, he started playing a song. The notes rang out sweetly into the air. Annabelle closed her eyes and listened as he played. When she opened her eyes again, the sun had disappeared, and the stars were starting to shine through the darkness.

All the Gypsies were sitting around the fire now. As the old man finished one more song on his guitar, Anton broke the silence. "Gypsies have a stereotype of being unpredictable, sneaky, and untrustworthy characters." He paused to take a drink of wine out of a bottle. "But really, we are just passionate people. We are pretty predictable and straightforward. Do us wrong, and we will return the favor. Make us angry, and our rage will burn. Family is everything, and we will always stay true to our word. We know what we want, and we take it. This is the Gypsy way."

"Here here!" one of the Gypsy men said, raising a wine bottle in the air. The other Gypsies echoed "here here" and raised their bottles as well.

The old man with the guitar began playing again, and the younger Gypsies, men and women, began dancing around the fire singing songs that Annabelle had never heard before. She caught herself smiling as she watched a couple of the children dancing playfully with Rosie and Cleo. For a moment Annabelle let herself forget about the danger of the forest, the worries of her two worlds, and just soaked up the smell of the campfire and the laughter of the Gypsy group.

Nick stood up and, taking Annabelle's hand, they joined in the dance. She was so happy to hold his hand in her own and twirl to the music of the guitar. When Nick held her close, her heart swelled with happiness. Annabelle watched as Gary, Merry Anne, and her mom joined in as well.

As Nick twirled Annabelle, the wagon covered in cages caught her eye. Whatever was in the cages was glowing. Vibrant pink, purple, and yellow lights were streaming through the bars of the various cages. Nick followed her gaze to the cages.

"Don't focus on it," Nick whispered, turning Annabelle so her back faced the cages.

Annabelle wanted to ask why, but the music had slowed, and she realized that the Gypsies were dispersing and heading to their wagons for the night.

"You may sleep by the fire. Here are some blankets," Anton said, handing them to Nick. "One of us will keep an ear out, in case any of you . . . need anything."

"Thank you," Gary said, shaking Anton's hand.

As the group lay down, Merry Anne on one side of Annabelle and her mom on the other, Annabelle listened to the eerie silence of the forest. She closed her eyes and listened, waiting to hear the grunting of the trolls stomping through the forest or the howling of the wolves. The silence was deafening; not even a bug was singing tonight.

She rolled over to see whether Merry Anne was still awake, but she was no longer beside Annabelle. Merry Anne had silently slipped away from the group. Annabelle sat up and looked around, searching the clearing for her. The embers of the fire did not provide enough light for her to see. She let her eyes wander back to the wagon with the glowing cages on it. She could see someone standing in front of the cages.

Quickly, Annabelle stood up and walked over to the wagon. Merry Anne was standing in front of them, tears in her eyes.

"What is it?" Annabelle asked Merry Anne, putting her hand on Merry Anne's shoulder.

"The Gypsies are poachers," Merry Anne said, putting her hand on one of the cages. "But if we let the poor things go, they will come after us."

"Let what go?" Annabelle asked. The light glowing through the cages was so bright; she could not see what was trapped.

"Pixies," Merry Anne said weakly. "My mother used to tell me stories about them, but I have never seen one in all my years. And now, they are right here."

"Let's do it," Annabelle said, taking Merry Anne's hand. "We can let them go and get a head start out of here before the Gypsies even know we are gone."

Without waiting for a response, Annabelle opened up one of the larger cages. The sound of flapping wings broke the silence. Three little creatures flew out. Their glowing light hurt Annabelle's eyes. She squinted to try and get a better look at them. Their wings were almost like a dragonfly's. The pixies had human-like characteristics.

"What are you doing?!" Gary whispered behind Annabelle, startling her so much that she knocked one of the other cages over.

"They have trapped pixies," Annabelle said, looking around to see if the noise woke anyone.

"They will not be happy about this," Gary said.

"You know already they weren't going to let us go," Merry Anne said. "I heard the men talking."

Gary paused, looking at the pixies flying around the other locked cages. "You're right. We had better be leaving."

They worked quickly to open the other cages and let the pixies out.

Annabelle stepped back to watch the pixies as they flew together, merging to form one large pixie. She took another step back in awe of the sight and bumped into Nick. He and Annabelle's mother noticed Gary leaving and followed him to the wagon.

"Let's go," Nick said, handing Annabelle her pack.

Merry Anne scooped up Cleo.

"Thank you," the giant pixie said in a wispy voice, reaching her glowing hand out to the group. "For your help, we will get you out of the forest." They split back into small pixies, buzzing about the group like flies.

"HEY!" Anton shouted, running out of his covered wagon. His yelling roused the other Gypsies, who climbed out of their wagons as well. "Get them!" he yelled.

As the angry Gypsies headed toward Annabelle's group, Rosie nervously leaped into her arms. "What are we going to do?" Annabelle asked, looking to Gary.

It was then that she realized her feet were off the ground. The pixies had split up and picked Annabelle's mom, Nick, Gary, Merry Anne, and Annabelle up and were lifting them quickly, high into the air. Annabelle watched as the Gypsies disappeared out of sight. She laughed with relief, peering through the dark to look from face-to-face of each person in her group. Gary had a big smile on his face. "Oh, if Russell was not a toad, he would be panicked! He doesn't even like riding horses. He will never believe this!" Gary said, spreading his arms out into the air, feeling the wind rush past him. Annabelle thought about pulling Russell out of her pack, but she didn't want to risk dropping him or Rosie.

The pixies carried them over the trees of the Enchanted Forest. Their vibrant glowing lights pierced the darkness; they glowed brighter than the stars. As the sun started to rise, Annabelle could see creatures stirring down below through the trees. Birds flew by them, gawking at the group in confusion as they passed. She could see large, dark, four-legged animals running through the woods, but she couldn't quite see what they were.

When the sun had fully risen, the pixies dipped down into the forest, setting everyone's feet back on the ground. The pixies regrouped into the large pixie. "We are at the edge of the trees but cannot go any farther. The forest is our home."

"Thank you!" Merry Anne said smiling. "That was amazing!"

The group watched the pixies fly away through the forest until they could no longer see the colorful glow they emitted. As if a weight had been lifted, even the forest seemed less gloomy. They walked along the familiar root-riddled path they had come in on.

"They have to group together to talk. When they are small, their voices are too little to be heard," Merry Anne said smiling. "I can't believe we saw pixies."

It wasn't long until the group could see the light cutting through the forest. Annabelle's heart lifted; she knew she was almost home!

A dark figure stepped onto the path, blocking their way. It was one of the creatures Annabelle had seen running through the trees. A deep howl cut into the silence of the forest. The wolves had found them. His bright yellow eyes glared at the group. The wolf gnashed his teeth as the fur on his back rose.

Annabelle turned to see three more wolves join the one blocking the path. The wolves circled the group, inching closer and closer.

"Why can't we get a break?" Annabelle exclaimed. She was exhausted. The lack of sleep and the continuous struggles had worn her down.

Suddenly, two small creatures leaped out of the trees

onto the back of the wolf that had been standing in the path, blocking the way. They were beating the wolf with rocks and sharp sticks. The wolf howled and tried to roll them off. The wolf stumbled off the path and down the steep hill. Back on the path, rocks flew from above the trees, pelting the other wolves.

"We are here, Princess, we will hold them back!" a small voice squeaked, stepping onto the path beside the group. It was the same creatures that stole the wagon wheels off their wagon when the group first entered the forest—wood elves. The little elf boldly stood beside Annabelle, glaring at the wolves. The elf's bark-like skin blended in perfectly with the forest. Her grey eyes reminded Ann of the overcast sky.

The little elf brushed her moss-colored hair away from her face. She raised her hands and pointed them at the wolves. As Annabelle looked through the woods, she saw dozens of other elves in the trees. "Go, we will hold them back."

The group took off, running for the edge of the forest. They passed the last of the trees and were greeted by the light of the setting sun. Gary kept pushing them forward, and they kept running. Just when Annabelle didn't think her feet could carry her any farther, they saw a wagon heading toward them.

When the wagon reached the group, Annabelle was happy to see Jesse driving. "Surprised to see you here!" he called with a smile, climbing out of the wagon. He looked the group over. "Tangled hair, scratched-up skin, and ripped-up clothes. . . . Looks like you had that adventure you were wanting," he said with a grin. "Climb in, it will be a tight fit, but I will get you back to town. I was just dropping off one last delivery. People around here buy the goats we raise. I missed them at the farmer's market, so you were just lucky enough to catch me on a home delivery." Jesse brushed off the seat of the wagon and helped Annabelle onto it. "I don't have a lot of food, but please split it among yourselves. You all look hungry," Jesse said, handing Merry Anne two sandwiches and an apple.

"Why would the elves help us?" Annabelle asked curiously.

"Your magic," Merry Anne replied, smiling wistfully. "Wood elves are drawn to people with the most magic. Their life purpose it seems is to serve those with the most power."

Annabelle chewed on a fingernail in thought. She thought about how the elves served Raj, so why would they want to serve her now?

The group devoured the food Jesse gave them and then rode in silence the rest of the way home. They were too tired to talk, and everyone was ready to be safe at home. Jesse asked if they wanted to camp for the night, but Annabelle insisted they press on. She was anxious to get back to town. She kept trying to picture the look on her father's face when he saw her mom for the first time in so long.

As hard as Annabelle tried not to fall asleep, it wasn't long until she had dozed off in the wagon.

Chapter 22

Ann woke up in her bed as her alarm was going off. She pulled her blankets tightly around her, not ready to climb out of bed just yet. She ran through the events of everything that had happened in her father's world. "I am so close!" she said to herself, finally climbing out of bed.

She walked downstairs, looking for her mom. But she wasn't in the living room, or the kitchen. "Maybe she went to the store?" Ann asked herself out loud, shaking the worry out of her head that maybe, just maybe, her mom was still in the other world.

Digging for her cell phone in her purse, Ann called for Cleo. The house was silent, with no sign of Cleo either. Ann pulled her phone out of her purse and dialed her mom. As she waited for it to ring, she heard her mom's phone ringing in the kitchen.

Ann picked up her mom's cell phone, which was sitting on the counter. She could feel it in her stomach; she just knew her mom was still back in her father's world. Ann heavily sank into one of the kitchen chairs. She was fine being home alone, but to be alone in this world, that was a scary feeling.

Ann wandered around the house aimlessly. She wasn't sure what she should do. After several hours of attempting to take a nap on the couch with no luck, Ann stepped outside and sat in her mom's rocking chair. She looked out into the yard at the old oak tree. Closing her eyes, Ann listened to the birds singing. Ann alternated between sitting in the rocking chair and pacing the porch all afternoon. When her stomach finally started to growl, she gave up on trying to take a nap and went to make herself some lunch in the kitchen.

After lunch Ann aimlessly walked through the house. She sat in the den and tried to imagine it the way it was when her father still called this world his home. She thought of all the laughter that once filled the house, and how her mom had tried so hard to hide the sadness and pain once her dad was gone.

Ann spent the rest of the day in silence; she didn't even bother to turn the television on to help her feel less alone. She had too much to think through, she didn't want the distraction.

After microwaving and eating a TV dinner she had found in the freezer, Ann climbed into bed. Although it was only 7:30 PM, she thought she might be able to get to sleep, to get back to her family, to her other world.

Chapter 23

Annabelle stretched. Her back was sore from riding in the wagon. It bumped and jostled her around. As the sun rose, Annabelle was happy to see familiar sights of Emerson's Town. She scratched behind Rosie's ears, causing Rosie to wake up, open her eyes, and look around.

"We are here," Jesse said, stopping the wagon by the old white barn that was close to Emerson's farmer's market.

The group climbed out of the wagon. Annabelle pulled Russell-the-toad out of her pocket. "Gary, let's head to the dock," she said, handing Russell to him.

On the way to the dock, they stopped at the old barn and picked up two palomino horses. Annabelle tangled her fingers in the mane of one of the horses. It made her wonder, what happened to Lucy and Lace?

It didn't take long for Annabelle and Gary to get to the dock. Happily, Annabelle took her shoes off and ran to the end of the dock. Cattails lined one side of the water, peacefully swaying in the breeze. Rosie leaped off the dock excitedly into the water. Annabelle dipped her toes in. She looked carefully in Gary's hands at Russell-the-toad. Russell's eyes still looked like they were scowling. "Do you think this will work?" Annabelle asked hopefully, looking up at Gary.

Gary smiled. "There's one way to find out." He handed Russell to Annabelle. "Give him a toss."

Annabelle carefully dropped Russell into the water. She closed her eyes. She could feel the magic pulsing around her, flowing into the water.

"GIVE HIM A TOSS!" Russell shouted, his head breaking through the surface of the water. "You know I can't swim!"

Gary laughed, walking into the water. "It isn't that deep."

Russell frantically dog paddled to Gary, who handed him some pants. "I had a feeling you would be needing these," Gary said, chuckling.

"Thanks," Russell said, putting them on in the water. "I think I am done with these adventures."

Gary put his arm around Russell as they got back to dry land. "Glad to have you back, my friend," he said, smiling. "Let's get Annabelle home now."

When they got back to the barn, a carriage was waiting for them. Annabelle's mom was sitting inside with Cleo on her lap. "Merry Anne and Nick have already gone," she leaned over to tell Annabelle.

Annabelle was disappointed. She was hoping to thank them and tell them goodbye. As she loaded Rosie into the carriage, Russell tiredly looked at one of the palomino horses. "Princess. . . . I think I will sit this one out."

"Thank you, Russell," she said, hugging him tightly.

"I'm sorry you were a toad for most of the time."

"I guess it comes with the job," he said, shrugging his shoulders.

The trip home seemed to take forever. Annabelle couldn't wait to have her family all in one world! When the castle came into sight, she had the door to the carriage open and her feet on the ground before the carriage even came to a halt.

Her father was waiting for them, leaning against the old oak tree her swing hung from. He had a light in his eyes that she had never seen before. He scooped Annabelle up in his arms and swung her around in a big hug. "Welcome home," he told her, hugging her even tighter. "Did you get any answers? Merry Anne and Nick arrived before you but told me I had to hear the news from you."

Annabelle grinned. She broke the embrace and ran over to the carriage. There sat her mother, tears streaming down her face.

"Lori?" Annabelle's father asked in disbelief. "How?"

"James!" Annabelle's mother sobbed, stumbling out of the carriage.

They hugged affectionately, leaning against each other so hard it seemed that if one backed away, the other would crumble to the ground. He held her face in his hands, kissing her.

Annabelle's father refused to take his eyes off his wife, for fear she would disappear if he looked away.

"Lori?" Aunt Ester asked, stepping out of the castle. She broke into a run, first hugging Annabelle, and then Annabelle's mother. "Let's go inside, you guys must be starving."

Annabelle's heart was so full; her family was finally all together again.

"*The world's balance must remain even, for that, one must be leaving,*" Raj's voice echoed into her head.

Annabelle's heart sank. "No," she said in her head, picturing herself screaming it at Raj. "No, No, NO!" She held back the tears and forced herself to keep smiling. She wasn't going to ruin this moment, not now. In her heart, she wished that just ignoring Raj would keep her mother here.

"We must have a celebration," Aunt Ester said to Annabelle, interrupting Annabelle's train of thought. "We can invite the whole town! A big feast." Ester paused, putting her hand on Annabelle's shoulder. "I forgot, a couple from your traveling party is waiting for you in the barn."

Annabelle watched her father lead her mother into the castle, hand in hand. It was a bittersweet feeling, knowing they finally were together, only to be ripped apart again. She turned her eyes to the barn and with Rosie at her heels, she walked toward it.

Merry Anne's laughter echoed through the stalls, greeting Annabelle before she made it into the barn. She ran the rest of the way to her, excited to be able to thank her for everything.

"Welcome home!" Merry Anne called, giving her a hug.

"Thank you so much, Merry Anne," Annabelle said genuinely. "I am so grateful to everyone in the group."

"We were happy to go with you," Nick said, walking out of one of the stalls. "Look who we brought home." He was pulling a horse out of the stall behind him.

"Lucy!" Annabelle exclaimed, digging her fingers into her coat. "How did she find her way here?"

"Lace," Merry Anne replied, gesturing to the stall next to Lucy. "She always finds her way home. They both were in need of a bath and some water when they got back to town, but we got them cleaned up and here just in time to see you."

"Thank you so much," Annabelle said, hugging Lucy tightly around her neck. "I am so happy she's safe." Annabelle turned to Nick and Merry Anne. "We are going to have a big dinner tonight; you two must join us."

"We wouldn't miss it," Nick said, taking her hand in his. "Let's get you back to the castle."

When Annabelle and Nick found her parents, they were walking happily through the castle. Her father grinned brightly. "I've convinced Aunt Ester to just invite the group you traveled with to dinner tonight. I'd like to hear about your travels and have some time to talk with your mother. We will have plenty of time for celebrations and big feasts another day."

Annabelle nodded her head in agreement. She paused by the stairs leading to her room. "Can I show Mom?" she asked.

"Of course," her father replied.

Annabelle walked with her mom to her room. She showed her mother her favorite spot in the castle, the place where her adventures had begun.

Stepping out of the window of her room onto the roof, she gazed at the orange and red colors of the sky from the setting sun and looked over the rolling pastures. They watched the horses running through the tall grass and the peasants hustling about on the ground below. Glancing at her mother, Annabelle saw tears running down her face. "I can't believe this is all real. That your father is really here. Ester is really here. That I am really here." She paused, brushing a tear off of her cheek. "Maybe this is just a dream."

Smiling, Annabelle took her mom's arm and led her back into her room. Walking down the stairs Annabelle told her, "This is reality."

At dinner the group shared stories of their trip through the Enchanted Forest. Annabelle was pleased to see everyone there: Merry Anne, Russell, Gary, Nick, Aunt Ester, and her parents. Even Cleo and Rosie were chasing each other under the table and around chairs.

While they ate, Annabelle noticed that her parents were still holding hands. It was as if they were never going to let each other go. The group talked about the trip. Annabelle's father's laughter filled the room when he learned of Russell turning into a toad. Russell scowled, the same scowl that he had on his face when he was a toad.

As dinner finished up, Annabelle's father thanked them all for coming, and for their time spent on the journey. "Of all the blessings that I have been given, this is the greatest of all," he said, raising his hand that was entwined with Annabelle's mother's.

Annabelle's parents, Annabelle, and Aunt Ester sat around the table. The dining room seemed so empty without the rest of the group. Annabelle cleared her throat, deciding now would be the time to share the bad news. "Mom can't stay," Annabelle choked out, tears filling her eyes. "Raj gave us the necklace, but now she says that the two worlds are unbalanced if she stays." The words tumbled out of Annabelle's mouth.

Annabelle's father's smile faded. It was as if the weight of the world settled back onto his shoulders. "It is almost cruel. Dangle the chance of our family back together, only to take it away?"

"Let us make the best of it," Annabelle's mother said, taking her husband's hand back in her own. "We can't spend our last time together feeling sorry for ourselves," she smiled sadly.

"Come Annabelle; let's give them some time together," Aunt Ester said, standing up from the table.

Annabelle and Aunt Ester walked through the castle gardens, arm in arm. "You have grown so much my dear Annabelle," Ester said, patting Annabelle's hand with her own.

"Well, I am getting rather old," Annabelle smirked.

"No child, you have grown in spirit," Aunt Ester said, looking up at the stars gleaming in the jet-black sky. "You left a nervous little girl. You didn't just find your mother in your journey, but strength as well."

Annabelle smiled; a sense of pride grew in her. She had found herself on this trip. She faced trolls and Gypsies; creatures she didn't even know existed. She explored the unknown in creepy caves and flew in the air!

"You know, I had a life back in the other world. I had friends and a career . . . ," Aunt Ester trailed off, lost in her own thoughts. "It's getting late, we should get inside," Aunt Ester said, turning back toward the castle.

Annabelle met her parents as she was heading to her room. She hugged them both closely. Annabelle closed her eyes, savoring the embrace. She remembered as a child, before her father would go to work, the three of them would hug, Annabelle in the middle, to make an Annabelle sandwich. She wished this could last forever.

"Good night, Mom and Dad," Annabelle said, holding back her tears again. She stumbled up the stairs, crawled into bed, and cried herself to sleep.

Chapter 24

"*Open your eyes and say your goodbyes, your time here ends with the sunrise,*" Raj's voice echoed into her head.

Ann opened her eyes and sat up in the bed. Her heart felt heavy. "So, this is it," Ann thought to herself. "I'm going to lose my mom." She went downstairs and stood on the porch, looking into the yard at her beat-up old pickup truck. "Will anyone ever drive you again?" she asked out loud.

"I will be happy to."

Ann paused, not trusting her ears. She turned to see who was speaking. "Aunt Ester?" she asked in disbelief.

Aunt Ester smiled, sitting down beside Ann. "Yes, it's me. You can close your mouth now dear, it's not very ladylike." Aunt Ester took a deep breath, inhaling the fresh air. "After your mother went to bed, I snuck in and took her necklace. I figured it was the key to traveling." She pulled the necklace out from beneath her shirt, showing it to Ann.

"But now you will be stuck here," Ann said. "What will

you do in this world?"

Aunt Ester grinned. "I have a pretty amazing convertible in storage here; I have had countless dreams of taking it for a spin again."

Ann laughed, trying to picture her aunt driving around in a convertible, letting her hair blow in the wind. Ester seemed happier, more laid back in this world than in her father's. After a moment, her smile faded. "But what will my dad do without you?"

"With your mom there now, he will be just fine," Aunt Ester said, as she stood up from the rocking chair. "Now don't you have anything you'd like to do here?"

"I would like to visit some of my friends; it sounds like this will be my last time here," Ann said, standing up and stretching. "Would you like to come along?"

Aunt Ester smiled. "Thanks sweetie, but I will let you have your time to say your goodbyes. I think I will do some exploring here, see what has changed since I've been gone."

"Thanks, Aunt Ester," Ann said, hugging her tightly. "I'm going to change and head uptown."

Ann jogged up the stairs, pausing part way up. The thought that this might be one of the last times she is in this house weighed heavily on her shoulders. Her mom would never be back here to sit on their front porch. Lucy would never walk through their pasture, and Cleo would never sleep on her pillow in this house again. Tears stung her eyes as she jogged up the rest of the stairs to her room.

Quickly, Ann changed her clothes and sent a text out to her friends to meet her uptown. As she hurried out to her truck and started the drive into town, her mind wandered to Aunt Ester. She would be alone in this world once Ann was gone.

As Ann pulled into an empty parking space, she saw her friends waiting for her under a tree that sits in front of Dirksen's Café. She climbed out of the truck and joined them. There was a slight breeze that rustled the leaves. The group headed inside.

The group placed their ice cream orders and then sat down in a large booth in the little loft. The day went by quickly, everyone talking about going off to college and the adventures that awaited them. As sad as Ann would be to say goodbye to her friends for the last time, she was happy. Everyone had their own adventure to embark on. Noah was going to college for engineering, Grace to be a biologist. Megan was going to become a teacher. Ann did not share that she was going to be a princess. Her friends all had their dreams. As everyone talked about their campus visits and getting settled into their dorms, Ann listened quietly.

"I should probably be heading home," Ann said, standing up from the booth. "I am really going to miss you guys."

"We will get together on breaks!" Grace said, smiling as she hugged Ann tightly.

"About that . . . ," Ann said, looking back to the rest of the group. "My mom and I, we are going out of the country. I—I'm not sure for how long. My Aunt Ester will be taking care of the house while we are gone."

Noah stood up, giving Ann a hug. "We will see you when you're home then." He hugged Grace and Megan and paid for everyone's ice cream before leaving the café, Grace following shortly after him.

Megan hugged Ann goodbye. "Good luck on your new adventure," she said, picking up her purse and leaving the café.

Ann stood inside the café by herself for a moment. It seemed like just yesterday she was having lunch with her mom here, talking about the other world. And now, her mom was with her dad in that world. She shook the thoughts out of her head, took a deep breath, and walked back to her truck.

Aunt Ester was proudly buffing a cherry-red convertible as Ann pulled into the drive. Her silver-grey hair was freely blowing in the wind. Ann had never seen Aunt Ester's hair down before; for as long as she could remember it was tightly pinned back in a bun. Aunt Ester seemed completely different, no longer the uptight woman who lived in the castle, but a woman ready to enjoy the world.

As Ann climbed out of the truck, Aunt Ester greeted her with a warm smile. Her eyes were shining with happiness. "Just as beautiful as when I left her!" Aunt Ester said, gesturing toward the car. "I wonder why your mom didn't drive her around." Ester tossed the old towel she was using to buff the car to the ground. "Let's go inside for a bit. I saw some lemonade in the fridge."

Ann nodded in agreement, following her inside.

Aunt Ester poured them each a glass and sat down at the table across from Ann. She studied Ann's face, took a sip of lemonade, and then sighed. "I don't like to share stories of the past, but I think it is time." Smiling sadly, Aunt Ester continued, "In the other world, I had fallen in love. It was easy for me to stay there when my traveling came to an end. Yes, I had friends here that I have missed—I can't wait to see the look on their faces when I show up at their door. But when my high school sweetheart in this world went away to college, I thought I was meant to be with Logan. We were planning to marry and have more children than the castle could hold." She laughed to herself at the thought of this. As her smile faded, she continued, "But one day when he was out in the woods with a hunting group, they were ambushed by trolls. Few from the group made it back. They carried with them the news that Logan would never return." Aunt Ester twisted her mouth, fighting back the sadness in her voice.

"I am so sorry, Aunt Ester," Ann said, taking Ester's hand in her own.

"I never wanted a life in that world after that. So much of me wondered, if I had picked this world instead, maybe he would still be alive." She shook her head, as if to brush the thought away. "But now, I can have a fresh start. I will take great care of everything here. Please tell your mom—never will a weed flourish in her gardens." Aunt Ester patted Ann's hand and stood up from the table. "Now, best you head to bed. A new adventure awaits you."

"Thank you, for everything," Ann said, hugging her aunt tightly. "You will always be in my heart."

Ann climbed the stairs to her room, stopping part way to look at her living room once more. She smiled, imagining Nick and the rest of the crew all piled into that room. She had always wanted to have a big adventure and leave this little town, but she never realized how much she truly loved this home.

The sound of a car pulling into the driveway caught Ann's attention. She peeked out her bedroom window to see Officer Andrews's police car. Ann smiled to herself. At least now she knew Aunt Ester will not be alone in this world.

The front door swung open and Aunt Ester walked out to the driveway. She didn't even have her shoes on. Officer Andrews climbed out of his police car faster than Ann had ever seen him move. They stood and stared at each other, only for a moment, before Aunt Ester ran to meet him. He wrapped his arms around her, and they kissed. Ann was almost embarrassed to be watching and closed her curtain. She knew Aunt Ester would have love and happiness in this world; she was going to be okay.

Curling up into her bed for the last time, Ann bunched the pillow up under her head. It was a strange feeling; she didn't have to share the bed with Cleo. After a lot of tossing and turning, Ann finally got her restless mind to go to sleep.

Chapter 25

Annabelle woke up and stretched. Her hands knocked into Rosie and Cleo, who were curled up on opposite sides of Annabelle, frowning at each other. Annabelle laughed, running her fingers down the backs of both of them. "You guys are just going to have to get along," she said, swinging her feet off the end of her bed.

The thought of Raj flashed through her mind. Part of Annabelle felt sorry for her. Raj was alone in this world; she had no one. Annabelle paused, closing her eyes. She pictured Raj's grey-green eyes and curly grey hair. Annabelle felt her skin grow hot, her veins burning with magic. Suddenly, the empty black behind Annabelle's eyelids swirled into a fog, and soon she was looking into Raj's cottage, in her kitchen. Raj was sipping a cup of tea as she gazed out the kitchen window, watching the wood elves work in her garden.

Raj paused in mid sip, looking around her kitchen. "Who dares to eavesdrop on me?" she asked, putting her cup and saucer down. Raj slowly walked through the room, carefully looking around. "Oh, little Princess. Your young magic grows, but you have much to learn."

Surprised, Annabelle spoke: "Yes, Raj. I am here. I can see you."

Raj grinned as she picked up her cup of tea. "And I can sense that your mother is still in this world as well. You are a clever little witch."

"That was not my doing; it was my Aunt Ester's decision."

"Ah yes, Ester," Raj said, taking a drink of her tea. She let out a loud sigh. "She will find happiness in that world. As for you, I plan to see a lot more of you. With great magic comes great responsibility. The first thing I will teach you is how to knock before looking in on me again."

Annabelle smiled. "Fair enough, Raj. But with that, I have something to teach you."

"And what would that be?" Raj asked, raising an eyebrow.

"The value of family. You said your brother picked love and 'wasted' his magic. If you want to be my mentor in magic, I want to show you what it is to truly be a part of our family, to know love."

"I am open to this idea; it might be nice. But that is a discussion for another time. Get out of here and go see your parents," Raj said.

"Yes, ma'am," Annabelle said. Annabelle opened her eyes and watched the golden glow in her veins slowly fade back to normal. She stretched once more and then climbed out of bed. She quickly petted both Cleo and Rosie before leaving her room to go find her parents.

Her parents were already up when Annabelle reached the foyer. She could hear their laughter coming from the dining room. She stopped in the doorway to watch them together. They were holding hands while they were eating breakfast. Her parents were like newlyweds, still unable to let go of each other.

Annabelle's father caught sight of Annabelle. He stood from his chair and walked toward her. "Your Aunt Ester. I—"

Annabelle smiled sadly, hugging him. "I know, she is back in the other world, cleaning up her cherry-red convertible."

Annabelle's mother laughed. "I kept up the maintenance on that car for years. I always thought I was crazy for doing it, but part of me just knew she would come back for it someday."

"I can't believe you never let me drive it!" Annabelle said, scowling at her mom.

"An eighteen-year-old driving that? Yeah right!" she said, shaking her head. "That's why I hid it in the barn for so long. I didn't want either of us to put too many miles on Ester's pride and joy," her mom said, hugging Annabelle tightly.

"Your mother and I would like to go on a horseback ride, maybe show her around Emerson's Town and the farmer's market," Annabelle's father said. "Would you like to join us?"

Annabelle grinned, her heart never feeling so full. "I would love to."

As they headed toward the barn, a crisp breeze greeted them. "It will be a beautiful day for a ride," Annabelle's father said, leaning down to scratch Rosie behind the ears.

Merry Anne and Nick were in the barn, deep in conversation, as Annabelle and her family approached.

Annabelle's heart was in her throat; she was so happy to see Nick again. She couldn't wait to look into his handsome eyes. As soon as Nick caught sight of her, his face lit up. He grinned and walked quickly over to her.

"Good morning, Annabelle," Nick said, bowing to greet her.

Annabelle wrapped her arms around him and hugged him tightly.

"We will saddle the horses," Annabelle's father said to Nick, as he guided Annabelle's mother and Merry Anne toward the stalls, away from Nick and Annabelle. He gave Nick a wink as he walked past.

"I haven't been able to stay away from Pelland," Nick said with a smile. "Every excuse I had to come; I did." He held Annabelle's hands in his, kissing the tops of them.

"I can't wait to see what our future holds," Annabelle said with a smile. "I hope it includes many more adventures."

Nick grinned, "Maybe with a few less trolls."

"It's a deal," Annabelle said, giving Nick one more hug before she headed to the stalls to join her parents.

The horses were saddled and ready to go. Annabelle climbed on the back of Lucy and followed her parents out of the barn and through the pasture that led out of the castle grounds. Annabelle and her parents spent the day riding trails around the town. Her father proudly showed them more of their village and introduced Annabelle's mother to some of the people that were out working. Lucy happily sniffed the new surroundings; it was a whole new world to explore.

As the sun started to set, they returned home for dinner. "I will quickly wash up and be down," Annabelle called as she hurried to her room. She washed her hands and face in the water basin and pulled Aunt Ester's mink shawl over her shoulders.

When she got back down to the dining room, she was greeted by a full table. Annabelle's parents, Nick, Russell, Gary, Merry Anne, Whitney, and many more people filled the room. Annabelle smiled in surprise.

"We have to hear more stories of your trip," her father said, gesturing to the crowded group.

"Well, it's a good thing there's plenty of food, because this could take a while," Russell said, taking a massive bite out of a dinner roll. "Just no talk of toads," he said while chewing.

Taking a seat between her mother and Nick, Annabelle smiled. It was then that she realized how much she had grown. No longer was she the nervous child who had gotten blown out of her bedroom window clutching a paisley umbrella. No longer was she a caged soul who envied her free horses. She was a strong woman who battled trolls and wolves. Magic flowed through her veins, and someday she would be powerful.

It was late in the night when the chatter died down and people slowly dispersed. After the food had disappeared and the candles were burning low, it was just Annabelle and her parents left at the table. Annabelle promised to always remember this night, a wonderful celebration of love and adventure.

Annabelle stifled a yawn as she stood up from the table. "I am going to bed as well." She stretched and looked at her parents one more time. "Good night, Mom and Dad." She turned and walked to her room, with Rosie at her heels.

As Annabelle climbed into bed, she pulled a corner of her pillow out from under a scowling Cleo and curled up under her heavy quilt, with Rosie pressed tightly beside her. She closed her eyes and let out a loud sigh. Finally, she was at home with her whole family. And for the first time in forever, Annabelle not only slept, she dreamed.

About Atmosphere Press

Atmosphere Press is an independent full-service publisher for books in genres ranging from nonfiction to fiction to poetry, with a special emphasis on having an author-friendly approach to the challenges of getting a book into the world. Learn more about what we do at atmospherepress.com.

We encourage you to check out some of Atmosphere's latest releases, which are available at Amazon.com and via order from your local bookstore:

Carpenters and Catapults: A Girls Can Do Anything Book, children's fiction by Carmen Petro

Owlfred the Owl, a picture book by Caleb Foster

Mere Being, poetry by Barry D. Amis

Mandated Happiness, a novel by Clayton Tucker

The Third Door, a novel by Jim Williams

The Yoga of Strength, a novel by Andrew Marc Rowe

They are Almost Invisible, poetry by Elizabeth Carmer

Let the Little Birds Sing, a novel by Sandra Fox Murphy

Spots Before Stripes, a novel by Jonathan Kumar

Auroras over Acadia, poetry by Paul Liebow

Channel: How to be a Clear Channel for Inspiration by Listening, Enjoying, and Trusting Your Intuition, nonfiction by Jessica Ang

Gone Fishing: A Girls Can Do Anything Book, children's fiction by Carmen Petro

Love Your Vibe: Using the Power of Sound to Take Command of Your Life, nonfiction by Matt Omo

Transcendence, poetry and images by Vincent Bahar Towliat

Leaving the Ladder: An Ex-Corporate Girl's Guide from the Rat Race to Fulfilment, nonfiction by Lynda Bayada

Adrift, poems by Kristy Peloquin

Letting Nicki Go: A Mother's Journey through Her Daughter's Cancer, nonfiction by Bunny Leach

Time Do Not Stop, poems by William Guest

Dear Old Dogs, a novella by Gwen Head

Bello the Cello, a picture book by Dennis Mathew

How Not to Sell: A Sales Survival Guide, nonfiction by Rashad Daoudi

Ghost Sentence, poems by Mary Flanagan

That Scarlett Bacon, a picture book by Mark Johnson

Such a Nice Girl, a novel by Carol St. John

Makani and the Tiki Mikis, a picture book by Kosta Gregory

What Outlives Us, poems by Larry Levy

Winter Park, a novel by Graham Guest

That Beautiful Season, a novel by Sandra Fox Murphy

What I Cannot Abandon, poems by William Guest

All the Dead Are Holy, poems by Larry Levy

Rescripting the Workplace: Producing Miracles with Bosses, Coworkers, and Bad Days, nonfiction by Pam Boyd

Surviving Mother, a novella by Gwen Head

Who Are We: Man and Cosmology, poetry by William Guest

About the Author

Jennifer Deaver was born and raised in a small town in Iowa. She lives on an acreage with her husband, two children, a rat terrier, and several cats. She enjoys spending time with her family, being outdoors, and working on numerous art projects. Jennifer started writing stories in an attempt to spark her son's interest in reading.

She lovingly uses family members and friends as characters throughout this book, and she even uses some of her own life experiences. Jennifer's love of reading and desire to encourage others' imaginations motivated her to set her fears aside and publish her story. This is her first novel. She is excited to show her children that dreams do come true!